Dead Man's Money

K. J. North

Enjoy the read !
K. J. North

Copyright @ 2021

Author's Note

All rights reserved. No part of this book may be reproduced or transmitted in any form, including photocopying, recording, or other electronic or mechanical methods, without permission in writing from the publisher. The exception would be for the use of quotes or citations in a book review.

K. J. North has written this book as a work of fiction. Names, places, and events are either products of the author's imagination or are used fictitiously.

About the Author

K. J. North is a suspense fiction writer who resides in a small town on the Oregon coast. In addition to writing, she enjoys spending time with family, traveling, and experiencing everything related to creative art. She and her husband own a vacation rental and love hosting guests from all over the world.

On an average day, you might find her writing or walking the beaches and collecting pebbles for her pebble art.

K. J. North
http://kjnorth.com/
Contact K. J. North
Sign up for K. J. North's newsletter

Dead Man's Money: A Troy and Eva Winters Private Investigation Thriller, Book 2

Private Investigators Troy and Eva Winters are thrilled when Troy's sister, Sadie, announces that she and her family are moving to Elk River, only a twenty-five-mile drive from New Haven, where Troy and Eva live. Now Sadie will be close to her family and, with their support, can try to overcome her debilitating panic disorder of agoraphobia.

Troy's joyful Christmas holiday is suddenly shattered when he receives a cryptic message from his ten-year-old niece, Willow. Her cry for help and the startling message—"The bad guys are here"—send Troy's distress alarm into overdrive. It does not take him long to realize the deadly consequences that lie ahead.

With Eva out of town, Troy sets out for Elk River on his own with no idea of the danger he'll soon face. He's close enough to Willow to know the threat is real, and the urgency in her voicemail message confirms it. Just when a flicker of hope appears, Eva goes missing. Time is not on Troy's side, and the clock is quickly ticking down on any chance of finding his wife alive.

See all of K. J. North's books at:
http://kjnorth.com/available-books/

Find K. J. North on Facebook at:
https://www.facebook.com/kjnorthauthor/

Don't want to miss K. J. North's next release?
Sign up for the newsletter at:
http://kjnorth.com/newsletter/

Chapter 1

The sound of small, shuffling feet woke him. Peering through his slightly opened eyes, Oliver watched as the silhouette of four-year-old Finn got closer to his side of the bed. Finn was haloed by the bedroom nightlight, which sent an eerie glow around his small body.

If I keep my eyes closed and don't move, will he go away?

"Daddy, Daddy, wake up."

"Finn, why are you in here? Remember, we want you to stay in your bed until it gets light outside. Then you can come in and wake Mommy and Daddy up."

"The bad guys are here. I wanted to tell you that the bad guys are trying to get in the house."

Sadie rolled over in bed, probably to see what was going on. "Finn, what's the matter? Do you remember what Mommy said? You should be used to sleeping in your own room now."

"I *was* getting used to sleeping in my own room, Mommy, but the bad guys woke me up."

Sadie let out a sigh. "See, Oliver, we should have turned the channel to something more kid friendly when he walked into the living room last night."

"Sorry, I didn't think he'd take note of the movie that much. He was playing with his new Christmas toys on the floor. Come here, Finn. Crawl in between us, and let's all go back to sleep." Oliver pulled aside the blankets so Finn could crawl over.

Finn was having none of that, though. He wanted Daddy to make the bad guys go away.

"Okay, get in here, and I'll go chase them off, and then we'll all go back to sleep." He glanced at the illuminated clock on the nightstand—5:44.

Oliver walked out of their bedroom and was ready to turn in to the bathroom when he decided to glance in Finn's bedroom first. That way, he wouldn't be lying to his son when he got back in bed and told him that the bad guys were gone. All was clear, of course. Oliver made his trip to the bathroom and snuggled back in bed with his wife and son, hoping for another hour or so of rest.

His wish came true as he drifted off to sleep until wakened by the light coming in through the crack in the curtains.

Saturday. No hurry to get up. I'll just relax for a bit and then surprise the family by making waffles and bacon for breakfast.

A few minutes later, he heard ten-year-old Willow's bedroom door open. He listened to her footsteps going down the stairs and wondered what woke her. She was at that age where she usually slept in until later in the morning.

The next sound he heard—Willow screaming—made him jump out of bed and run.

"Dad, Dad, what are they doing here?"

He raced down the steps then came to a sudden stop when he saw why Willow was screaming. Two men wearing ski masks sat in the living room, one of them with a gun pointed at her.

"What are you doing here? What do you want? Get the hell out of my house." Oliver grabbed Willow around the waist and pushed her toward the steps. "Go upstairs and stay there."

"You said that wrong, Oliver. I ask the questions from now on. Call your wife and kids down here, now," said the tall man wearing glasses. He stood and walked toward the steps.

"Like hell I will."

It was too late. Sadie was already running down the stairs, her eyes wide with fear. Finn and Willow were right behind her. She looked at the men and screamed, "How did you get in? Get out of here before I call the police!"

The tall man laughed at her. "Like I said, I ask the questions, and I call the shots. And as you can see, I've got the gun. Now let's try this again. First question, where are your phones?"

Oliver took a couple of steps toward the man. "None of your damn business. What the hell do you want here?"

"You've got one minute, or my friendly associate will escort your wife to find them."

The other man stood up. He was short and heavyset.

Finn broke loose from his mom's grasp and ran to his dad. He clenched his fists at his side and screamed, "My dad will beat you up and take you to jail, you bad guys!" It was his four-year-old way of telling them off.

For a few uneasy seconds, the tall man locked eyes with Finn, then he shook his head and sighed. He looked over at the other man, who leaned against the living room wall. "Take the wife upstairs and find the phones. Look in the kids' rooms too. These days, all kids have phones."

The shorter man walked over and reached out as if to grab Sadie when Oliver yelled, "Stop! I'll tell you. My phone is probably on my desk upstairs in my office, and Sadie usually keeps hers in her office, which is the room next to the kitchen. The kids don't have phones."

"See? When you cooperate, life can be a little more pleasant."

The shorter man looked at the tall man with the gun, who gave him a nod.

"Go ahead. Get the phones, and check the kids' rooms, anyway. Destroy any computers or laptops you see up there, anything that can get a signal out."

Oliver held onto Finn and stood in front of Sadie and Willow, trying to protect them. His mind raced, wondering how he could get the gun away and keep his family safe.

A few minutes later, the shorter man came back in the living room with two phones and a laptop and threw them on the floor. "I destroyed the upstairs computer and cut the Wi-Fi line. I'll check the rest of the house and the garage," he said as he walked away.

The tall man paced the room. "Okay, it looks like things are going in the right direction. Now, I want all four of you to have a seat on the couch."

"What do you want with us? You need to leave now!" Oliver ordered.

The man took a few steps toward him and pressed the gun barrel against the side of Oliver's head.

Sadie screamed, and the kids were crying. "Stop. We'll sit down, just leave us alone," Sadie pleaded. She took hold of Willow's hand and led her to the couch. Then she begged Oliver, "Please, let's just do it and see what they want."

Oliver did as his wife asked, holding tightly onto Finn.

The man lowered his gun. "That's more like it. Now I only have one question, and I better get a good answer. Where's the money?"

"What money?" Oliver gave the man a stern look. "I don't know anything about any damn money."

"Wrong answer." Again, the man pointed the gun at Oliver then grabbed Sadie by the arm and yanked her up off the couch.

Oliver screamed, "Stop!" and jumped to his feet.

The kids' cries got louder. The man switched the gun to the side of Sadie's head, and his other hand went tightly around her waist, forcing her to hold still.

"Our wallets are upstairs, and we don't have a safe. Take whatever you can find and get the hell out of here," Oliver said.

"One more time, if you want your wife to live, I'll tell you exactly what money. The money that Lucas kept here. Where's the one million four hundred thousand dollars?"

Chapter 2

Three months earlier

Eva potted flowers on the deck as her husband walked up the steps, ready to take a break.

"All this yardwork is exhausting." Troy pulled off his work gloves and took a seat on a padded deck chair. "Great, you've got a pitcher of lemonade out here. I had a feeling you would. Thanks, babe."

"Sure, I was getting ready to call you but didn't think you'd hear me over the noise of the Weed eater. Let's sit down and relax a bit."

Eva poured two glasses of ice-cold lemonade and handed him one. She took a seat on the lounge and propped her legs up. "How's it going? Are you almost finished?"

Troy put the glass to his lips and took a couple of swallows. "Almost. Just a little bit more around the driveway and I'll be done."

Eva put her head back and relaxed, enjoying the warmth of the sun on her face. She thought back to the day they'd moved there. It was hard to believe it had already been three years. In her will, Eva's mom had left them the beautiful Frank Lloyd Wright–inspired bed-and-breakfast inn. Eva missed her mother every day and wanted to keep the place in impeccable shape, the way that her mom had. They were doing their best to take care of the inn and keep up with their part-time private investigation business in Portland, Oregon.

"Sadie called while you were out in the yard. I told her you'd call her back. We talked for a while, and I was happy to hear that they want to leave the city and come live down this way. She said they'll be moving back into their house in Gold Mountain. They already gave their renter a six-month notice."

"They are? That's great. We can be close to my sister's whole family again. Remember how much fun we had with the kids?" Troy stood up and refilled his glass.

"Yeah, it's been a while since we've seen them. Little Finn is four, and Willow must be, what, ten years old by now? Sadie said they couldn't handle the city anymore. After the virus, and with everyone in the stay-at-home way of life, she realized how much living out in the country again would mean to them as a family." Eva rose from her lounge and put her gardening gloves on. She pressed the potting soil down in the pot around the dahlias that she had just transplanted.

"Did she mention how she's coping with the agoraphobia?"

"No, she was quiet about it, but she did say that she was still going to have video chat appointments with her therapist. Of course, Oliver will do the driving to get down here. He'll do everything that needs to be done outside. The rest of the family just wants to help her and hope that things will get better."

Eva lined the flowerpots up close to the railing and looked at the beautiful view of the beach below.

Troy stood and put his arm around her. "We'll help them as much as we can. Just the little bit I've read about it, it sounds like a panic disorder. It all started when Dad got sick with the coronavirus. When he died, Sadie showed signs of being unable to leave the house. A week later, the phobia overcame her. It was all so sudden."

The French doors opened, and Jasmine appeared, her long blond hair pulled up into a ponytail. A checkered dish towel was thrown across her shoulder.

"Good morning, friends." Jasmine had moved in with them last year when she became the inn's chef. Jasmine had arrived in New Haven back then as a guest at the inn. She soon became good friends with Eva and Troy, and when she was kidnapped by a madman, they rescued her with the help of law enforcement. She had since become part of the family.

"Hey, Jasmine, good morning. Take a break and have some lemonade." Eva walked over to pour a glass of the cold drink for her friend.

Jasmine thanked her, sat down, and put her head back. "So, another beautiful day in New Haven. Blue sky and blue ocean. What more could we ask for? By the way, do we have any guests checking in this afternoon?"

Eva answered, "No, not until tomorrow. A couple from New Orleans will be coming in then and will stay until Friday. They should arrive midafternoon. Then on

Thursday, we have another couple coming in and staying until Sunday. I've got their names and information on my desk if you'd like to take a look."

"Okay, good. I'll plan the meals and go into town this afternoon to get groceries. Anyone want to take a morning walk on the beach with me?"

"Sounds like fun." Eva looked at Jasmine. "Low tide, what could be better?"

"You girls go ahead and have fun. I'll stay here and call my sister back."

Eva and Jasmine hiked down the trail to the beach as they had been doing together for close to a year. Low tide was the perfect time to go. They carried canvas bags to hold the shells and pebbles that looked like treasures to them. They walked along the water's edge, the seafoam tickling their ankles.

"Jasmine, do you know what agoraphobia is?"

"I sure do. I remember studying about it in psychology classes. Why, do you know someone who has it?"

"Yes, Troy's sister, Sadie. She had a light case of it when the coronavirus hit and everyone was in stay-at-home mode. But their father died of the virus, and then it just got worse for her. It's so bad now that she can't even go to the store. She has everything delivered. The walls of her house are her only safe haven."

Jasmine bent down and picked up some pebbles. She looked them over, kept two, then tossed them in her bag. "That's the worst case I've ever heard of. Poor woman. I wonder if the percentage of cases went up at the time the virus began to spread."

"They probably did. Anyway, we just got a message from her that she and her family are moving this way, into the house they used to live in. It's about half an hour from here. We're excited to have them live close by. In Seattle, it was too hard for the kids. No yard to play in. There was nothing for them to do but remain in the house during the stay-at-home order. At least down here, they'll have a yard, and she could watch out the window as they play."

"I'll be glad to meet her. Are they moving here soon?"

"I hope so. Troy is talking to her now, so maybe we'll know something more when we get back up to the house. I want to help them as much as possible. They've been through a lot."

Soon it was time to turn around and walk toward the trail to the house. Time to get back home and start their day.

Chapter 3

Sweat beaded up on Adam's forehead. It was unusually hot on that day in the middle of September, and the building was old. The air conditioner needed servicing once again. It was always something. Adam was getting tired of working at the Gold Mountain Federal Bank. He was thirty-eight years old and wanted some excitement in his life. Seeing all that money coming in and out was getting more and more tempting every day. He wanted something other than just the monthly salary from his position as bank manager. Half the time, he had nothing to do in the small-town bank, so he would help out the tellers at the counter.

"I'd like to deposit this," a woman said, interrupting his daydream.

Adam looked up to see Mary Fulton standing in front of him. "Yes, of course. How are you doing this fine day?" Not that he cared, but he had to make pleasant conversation to look like a trustworthy professional.

"I'll take eight hundred of that in cash, please."

Another check for ten thousand dollars to put in her account. Damn, how does she do it? She makes more money than I do. I know she's involved in some kind of online business where she just fools around at home on the computer each day and raises her kids while she's at it. Every month, she deposits at least this much.

"There you go." He counted out the eight hundred in cash. "And here's your deposit slip, Mary. Say hi to Sam and the kids for me."

In that backward town everybody knew everybody—and everybody's business. That was the bad part about wanting to do something illegal. Each day, when he saw the armored truck pull up, he knew that somehow, he would have that money as his own. Over the years, he'd gotten to know the drivers and their routes. Through the conversations, he picked up information about what banks they stopped at and how they sometimes diverted from their normal route.

It was time to get in touch with Gabe and Lucas, two longtime acquaintances that he'd gone to high school with. They thought like he did. For two years, they had talked about doing the deed, and it was time. The three of them lived hours from each other and kept in touch on burner phones. They were preparing for the time when something would go down. It wouldn't be good for them to be viewed as friends. If anyone was suspicious of one of them, the other two might be connected.

Glancing up at the clock, he saw that it was four forty-five. It was almost time to lock the doors and close out the tills. It was Friday, and he was dedicating his weekend to planning an armored car heist.

He had to laugh. *How many people think of that as they're going home on a Friday?*

"Hey, Adam, have a good weekend. I'm out of here." Abby grabbed her purse out of her locker and waved.

Trish was getting ready to leave, but she took her time. She was slow and more thorough about her closing duties. "Can I help you with anything before I go, Adam?"

"Thanks, Trish. I'm almost finished here. You go on home and get some rest. Put ice on that wrist of yours. I can tell it's been hurting you today."

"Yeah, arthritis. It's probably going to rain." She laughed. "Okay, then. See you Monday. I'll bring the doughnuts."

How many years has Trish been here? Probably twenty by now, and where has it gotten her? She was passed over for the position that I got and didn't even complain. She'll just go home to her average little house and her average little family and never have any real money.

Some people didn't care if they were ever rich, but Adam wasn't one of them. He secured the safe, grabbed his overcoat, and locked the bank doors on his way out to his new Denali. How many more payments did he have on that thing? He didn't want to think about it.

Twenty minutes later, he was in his apartment. He grabbed a beer out of the refrigerator, kicked back on the couch with his phone, and called Gabe. "Hey, it's Adam. What are you doing this weekend?"

"Hey, I haven't heard from you in a while. What's up, man?"

"I thought I'd drive over and hang out with you. I'll call Lucas and see if he can meet us there. It's time to plan what we've been talking about. No more waiting for me."

"Yeah, I feel the same way. I was looking forward to the day when we were actually going to sit down and figure out the details. Come on over. It's pretty quiet around here. No one is at the lake fishing, and nobody is hiking the trails now. I guess it's getting to be that time of the year. The schools are back in session, and vacations are over for people."

"Great, I'll see you early tomorrow afternoon. I'll make sure Lucas is on board." Adam ended the call and walked into the kitchen to see what was in the refrigerator for dinner. Leftover Chinese food. Good enough. He put it in the microwave and pressed Start. His next call was to Lucas. He hadn't seen him in a while. Lucas had moved away from the Portland area to live in some small town close to the coast.

After Adam tapped in his number, Lucas answered on the second ring.

"Hello?"

"What are you up to this weekend?"

"Adam, I figured it was you. Not too many people call me on this phone. This weekend? Hey, I'm doing whatever you're doing. I'm ready for that talk if that's what you're thinking."

Adam opened another beer. "You got it, man. I'm ready. I've been doing enough watching and planning in my head. Now it's time for action. I just talked to Gabe. He said it's pretty quiet around the cabin right now. I'll be there tomorrow afternoon."

"Great, I'll see you then."

The Chinese food filled him up, and Adam went to bed

early. The cabin was a three-hour drive southeast of his little town near Portland. In the morning, he wanted to take time to look over area maps and plot the route that the armored car drivers took.

The rain started in the middle of the night and was coming down heavy by daybreak. Thunder and lightning were unusual at that time of year and kept him awake. Adam got out of bed at five in the morning and looked over the route maps while he ate breakfast.

From what he'd learned, the truck stopped at three large banks before it arrived at his. There was never much money dropped at his bank, so by his estimate, they would be carrying a lot— over a million, probably a million and a half. The route to the next small-town bank was along a country road that he could view from the parking lot of his bank. As long as he and his friends came up with a plan to stop the truck, they could take the money and store it at Lucas's house until things quieted down. He would make sure no one touched the money or contacted each other for at least six months.

The drive to the cabin was unnerving. The road was winding uphill most of the way. Gusts of wind and intermittent downpours were steady. Water pooled up on the back roads as he got closer to the cabin. He heard a loud *crack* and looked up at the top of his windshield just as a tree began to fall across the road in front of him. Adam slammed on his brakes and swerved.

Chapter 4

As the SUV's front tires stopped within inches of the tree, Adam's breath caught in his throat.

A branch had jackknifed up and come to a landing on his windshield along with dirt and chips of bark.

What the hell. Damn, close call. That tree could have easily ruined my day and my life.

Adam sat there for a moment until his hands stopped shaking. He took out his phone and called Gabe. "Hey, I'm only about two miles from your cabin. A tree fell and missed me by a few inches. I even felt the bounce in my Denali when the tree hit the pavement."

"Damn. Well, I'm really not surprised with this weather. Sounds like a close call, though. So you must be okay since you're calling. How's the SUV?"

"Hang on." Adam got out and looked at the car. He found only a small dent on the front fender. "Okay, a branch ended up on my windshield, but nothing looks damaged. Just a small dent in the front. Doesn't look too bad. I'll consider myself lucky."

"You're two miles down this road? I'll be there with my chain saw in ten minutes."

Lucas arrived before Gabe even got there, and he pulled to a stop right behind Adam's SUV. He got out and walked over to the fallen tree as Adam cleared off the branch and debris from his windshield.

"Are you okay, man?" Lucas yelled over to Adam.

"Yeah, get in the car with me. Gabe's going to be here any minute with a chain saw."

They got out of the bad weather and in the front seat, where they talked over what had happened. "Good to see you, man. Looks like you had a close call. Was it already down?"

"No. If I had been going one second faster, I would've been under this thing. I even heard the crack as it was falling. All I could do was slam on my brakes and stay alive."

After hearing the roar of an engine, they looked up to see Gabe parking his truck on the other side of the fallen tree. He got out with his chain saw, and Adam and Lucas joined him. Gabe pulled the cord, and the saw rumbled into action, cutting the tree into movable pieces within a few minutes. When they had cleared the road, the three men drove their vehicles on to the cabin.

They parked close to the door and hurried inside to get out of the rain. Gabe offered them a drink. "Hey, guys, beer or something stronger?"

Adam and Lucas agreed on beer and took seats in overstuffed chairs around Gabe's roaring fireplace, warming up after their wet and cold ordeal.

Adam pulled a few pieces of paper out of his jacket pocket. "Okay, this is what we've been waiting for. I've been doing a lot of thinking. I've got the route figured out and approximately how much money they would be carrying after they leave my bank. It looks like on any given day, they should be hauling more than a million. Probably a million and a half. Split that three ways, and it will be a decent heist."

He gave each guy a sheet of paper with a route map drawn on it. "Burn these after you've memorized them. I put an *X* on the road that is the most rural and that I can actually see from the back of the bank building. Since we're up on a hill, I've got a good view of some of the roads below. The thing I've been worried about all this time is how to stop the armored truck. That tree just stopped me and caused me to get out. I'm thinking along those same lines."

"So what do you mean? How could a tree just be lying in the road at the perfect time?" Gabe asked as he got up and threw another log on the fire.

"What if you and Lucas already had the tree down in the woods next to the road? A small enough tree that you could both block the road with it but large enough that the armored truck is going to stop."

Lucas walked over to the fire. He rubbed his hands together and warmed them. "Okay, I think I see where you're going with this, but where should we park, and how will the timing work?"

"We have to go over the details for sure, but I know there's quad and motorcycle trails throughout those woods next to that road. I'm thinking of something like you guys parking on a road close by, on the other side of the woods. You would unload the quads, drive to the road that the truck is going to be on, and at my phone call, you two haul the tree across the road."

Gabe looked over the paper and glanced up at Adam. "So you're going to stand in the parking lot of the bank and watch then give us a call when it's time?"

"Yeah, I'll just wait for the ten minutes it would probably take for the truck to get there, and then I'll let the women know I'm going on a break. If you guys have any thoughts, let's hear them. I just wanted to run some ideas across."

Lucas and Gabe eyed each other, then Lucas shook his head. "I can't think of anything else, and this might really work. We knew we had to find some way of stopping them so they'd get out of the truck."

Gabe agreed. "You know, it sounds good. Let's work out the details of this plan. If all goes right, we might not even have to kill anyone."

Chapter 5

The day had finally come. They'd gone over the details until the plan was perfected. Gabe and Lucas were in the woods with their quads, just waiting for the call from Adam. Their trucks were parked on a logging road a mile away from where the heist would take place. After they got the money, they would drive the quads through the woods, ride them up the ramps and into the truck beds, cover them with tarps, and go their separate ways. The tree had already been cut and was lying along the side of the road at the exact place that it needed to be. They knew approximately what time the call would come in, but the timing had to be more exact. No vehicles could be traveling in front of the armored truck when they hauled the tree across the road. From Adam's vantage point on the hill in back of the bank, he would be able to tell when the truck was coming around the corner.

It had pulled up outside the bank right on time. William was driving, and Jackson brought in the sack of money. Adam spotted them out the window of his office. He made small talk with Abby and Trish and got the paperwork signed. Jackson was back out to the truck within a few minutes.

That morning, Adam had parked his car so that when it was time for the heist, he could lean against it, take a smoke break, and have a perfect view of the remote road below him.

I'll give it five minutes and then walk out to the parking lot.

He looked at Abby as she helped old man Lawrence cash his Social Security check. He didn't see Trish. A woman waited her turn at Abby's window. The door opened, and a local contractor walked in. Adam noticed Abby glancing at his office. Usually, he would help at the teller's window if a line started to form. He acted like he didn't notice. Those were the most important few minutes of his life, and he couldn't get caught up in waiting on customers. Adam was nervous. He had to get outside soon.

Where the hell is Trish? In the bathroom?

Finally, old man Lawrence was finished, and he stopped and waved at Adam on his way out the door. The woman walked up to Abby's window and started a transaction. The construction worker looked like he was antsy to get waited on and get back to work. The front door opened, and two people walked in. Adam saw Abby look over at his office again.

Damn, it's never this busy. I'll have to act like I'm sick and need some fresh air.

Adam pushed his chair back from his desk and put on his best "I feel sick" look as he started to walk to the lobby. Just then, Trish came in and opened up her window.

"Next person, please. May I help you?"

Relieved, Adam headed out the back door. After he hurried to his car, he leaned against it and lit up a smoke. The road below was empty. He took out his phone and tapped in Gabe's number. He waited until the perfect time to press the call button. Then he saw a black car driving on the road. His chest pounded as his heartbeat sped up. He kept an eye on the car and hoped it wouldn't interfere with the heist. As he continued to watch, the car passed around the corner. All was okay. The armored vehicle would be coming anytime. Finally, he saw it turn right onto the rural road. There was no one in front. Adam pressed the call button.

"Yeah."

"It's time."

His hands shook as he ended the call. Adam stomped his cigarette out on the pavement and took a deep breath. He had to appear calm before he could walk back in. He paced the parking lot for a minute. Of course, the area of the road the heist was going to take place on was out of his sight. He made sure the guys knew that the tree had to go down on the part of the road that was most secluded. There was nothing more for him to do except go in and finish the day.

Adam walked in the rear door of the bank and into his office. He put a few folders in front of him and pretended to work on something important, hoping that the women would leave him alone and not ask any questions. After picking up a pen, he began to doodle on papers to look like he was hard at work.

Trish walked up to his door. "Excuse me, Adam. May I talk to you a minute?"

Adam glanced up at her, hoping he had a normal look on his face.

What the hell does she want now?

"Yes, Trish. What is it?"

"I'm so sorry, but my wrist is hurting so much today. I was wondering if you would mind if I took the rest of the day off. Maybe if I go home and put an ice pack on it and take some more of my medication, I might feel better."

He breathed a sigh of relief. "Sure, that's fine. Go home and relax. I'm sure Abby and I can handle things here. It'll probably be slow the rest of the day."

He filed away the folders that he'd pretended to work on and walked out to help Trish count her drawer so she could leave. He engaged in small talk with the two women, wishing the day was over so he could go home and find out what had happened with the heist. He was sure the nightly news would be interesting.

"Well, thanks again," Trish said as she got her purse out of her locker. "I'm sure my wrist will be better tomorrow. See you guys in the morning."

When she opened the back door to go to her car, Adam heard the sirens.

Chapter 6

Finally, the day was over. Adam made sure he avoided the rural road area, even though curiosity was killing him. He drove directly to his apartment. The local news would start any moment. He grabbed a beer out of the refrigerator, turned on the TV, and sat down.

The newscaster came on. "Good evening. Shocking news out of a small town close to Portland today. One dead and another in critical condition after a shootout involving the robbery of an armored car. More after the break."

What? Adam choked on his beer, and it sprayed from his mouth.

Who was killed? What the hell! This was supposed to go smoothly. He stood up and began a frenzied walk around the apartment. *Damn!*

Once the commercial was over, the newscaster continued. "Our top news tonight. Outside of the small town of Gold Mountain, two armed guards driving an armored car were making their usual stops when something went terribly wrong. A motorist driving on the rural road outside of town came upon the scene of an armored car stopped in the middle of the road. One guard, the driver, was fatally shot, and the other is in critical condition. The only information we have at this time as to what might have happened is that they were both found outside of the truck, apparently to clear a downed tree from the road. The suspects have not been apprehended, but it has been reported that they made off with over one million dollars."

Adam didn't know who to call first, Lucas or Gabe. He decided on Lucas. He was always the easier one to talk to and more levelheaded. Adam punched in his number. Lucas picked up on the second ring.

"What the hell, man? I thought we agreed not to kill anyone. Tell me you're at home and you have the money."

"Yeah, I got the money, and I made it home without incident. Everything was going smooth until Gabe got gun happy. We came out of it with one million four hundred thousand dollars. So each of us gets just shy of four hundred sixty-seven thousand dollars."

Adam couldn't sit still and paced the room. Living in an apartment, he knew that he should keep his voice low, even though he felt like screaming. "So tell me what happened. How did it go down?"

"Everything was going as planned. The truck stopped because of the tree. We watched in the woods as they both got out to move it. We walked up with guns showing and made one of them open the back door. Gabe held his gun on them both while one of them tossed the bags out to me. I got the money on the quad and covered the bags with a tarp. The next thing I knew, I heard gunshots, and Gabe was running at me, yelling to get the hell out. We both got on our quads, drove to our parked trucks, and went our own ways."

"Why did he shoot? You guys already had the money. What happened to the plan of zip-tying the men and locking them in the back of the armored car?"

"That, I don't know. You'll have to ask Gabe. I was busy securing the bags of money in the quad. I just got home a few minutes ago and brought the bags in. The plan is to hide it in the house, then we all get together in six months to divide it and go our own ways, right?"

Adam poured himself a shot of scotch, slammed it down, and paced. "Yeah, that's the plan. I trust you, Lucas. I can't really say the same about Gabe. Don't forget that I saved your life many years ago. If you even have an inkling of a thought of disappearing, you won't get away with it. Gabe would find you, even if I didn't."

"I would never screw you over, and I'll never forget that you pulled me out of the rock quarry years ago when I was unconscious. I told you, man, I owe you."

"I'll call Gabe and find out what happened. Remember, do everything you normally do in your everyday life, and I'll contact you in six months."

Adam hung up and was ready to call Gabe when his doorbell rang. *Damn, who can it be? Is it the cops?*

He took a deep breath and tried to appear calm. He peeked out the crack in the living room blinds.

Girl Scouts? They still sell cookies door-to-door? Oh well, I need to act normal. It's the neighbor's kids. What could be more normal than talking to them?

Adam opened the door and put on his best smile. "Hi, girls. I hope you're selling my favorite kind."

"Hi, Mr. Kent. Would you like to buy some Girl Scout cookies?" the two little girls asked in unison.

"Sure, I'll take a box of the Thin Mints, and do you have the peanut butter sandwich cookies? I love those. If you do, I'll take two boxes."

He got the money out of his pocket, gave it to them, and told the girls to keep the change.

"Thank you, Mr. Kent," they said together in their singsong voices.

Adam closed the door and walked over to sit down on the couch. His eyes were fixed on the TV, wondering whether they would report anything else about the heist. Knowing he had to call Gabe to find out exactly what had happened, he picked up his phone and looked at it, stalling. He wasn't sure if he was ready for the gruesome details. Adam felt bad that the driver, William, was dead. Adam had known him for many years, and he had a family—a wife and two teenage kids. He wondered what condition Jackson was in.

It was no time to get sentimental. He had to expect bad things to happen if he wanted to get that kind of money. After tapping in Gabe's number, he waited.

"Hey, talk to me. Why did it go down the way it did?"

"We got the money, didn't we?"

"Yeah, but I thought we had a foolproof plan that didn't involve killing anyone."

"That's the way it was going. We had the money, we were

almost out of there, and then the stupid guy went for his gun. I shot him in self-defense, man. The other guy was going for a gun strapped to his ankle. I saw on the news that he was still alive."

"I'm not happy, put it that way. Just like I told Lucas, live your life like you do normally, and I'll contact you both in six months. That's when we'll divide the money and go our own ways."

He ended the call then continued to watch the news. Nothing else was said about the robbery. He could only imagine what Trish and Abby would be yapping about tomorrow. He didn't want to think about it. It would be best to concentrate on what he would do with the money. In a couple of months, he could fabricate a reason for moving out of the area, something feasible to tell his acquaintances. That way, it wouldn't be such a surprise when he left. He could give thirty days' notice to the bank and go anywhere he wanted. That $467,000 would be a good start.

Chapter 7

Two and a half months later

It was time to get on the computer and log in to the video session with her therapist. Sadie had been doing that three times a week for close to a year. Her agoraphobia was real. Sometimes, she got mad at herself for having it, knowing that logically, she was being ridiculous. Nothing would hurt her if she simply walked outside of her home. But the sweating and shortness of breath would overcome her. She would start shaking, and her heart would pound. The fear of losing control would be overwhelming.

"Hello, Dr. Appleton. Can you see me?" Sadie looked closely at the computer screen. Then she saw Dr. Appleton's image pop up.

"Yes, hi, Sadie. I can see you now. Okay, let's get started. How have things been going this week? Have you tried any of the assignments that I gave you?"

"As I've told you, it's hard living in the city. When I look out the window at the street, I imagine that if I go outside, there will be people walking up and down the sidewalks.

There will probably be crowds, and I won't have control of how close they get to me."

Seeing the doctor's image soothed her. It made Sadie feel like she was being helped and that someone understood, like maybe she wasn't crazy after all.

"Well, Sadie, tell me the steps that you have taken since we last talked and how you felt when you tried them."

She smiled with a sense of pride. "I did walk out on the balcony. After taking three deep breaths, I realized I didn't feel the urgency to run back in. I think I stayed out there for at least five minutes. I saw people walking on the sidewalks below, and I wasn't terrified, probably because I knew they couldn't get close to me. I have some good news, though, Doctor. We decided to move back to our house in Oregon. The kids need a backyard to play in. The city is no place for them to grow up."

"That's wonderful. I'm happy for you. When is the move going to happen?"

"We were going to wait a few months so that our renter would have a good amount of notice. But last week we got a phone call from one of his relatives. They wanted to let us know that he recently was killed in a car accident. They're moving his furniture and possessions out now. We decided to go ahead and move down soon, right after we pack up our house. We'll be spending Christmas in the country."

"I'm sorry to hear about your renter, but I am happy you're leaving the city. I want you to think about the physical aspect of travel during the move. Come up with a plan that you think will work for you, and we'll talk about it in our next session."

"I will. I'll give it a lot of thought. Thank you."

Just then, Finn darted into the kitchen after one of his runaway toy trucks. Sadie grabbed him and gave him a big hug. She hadn't seen him yet that morning. She was happy that her son would soon have a yard to play in. He could build roads in the dirt to run his trucks on. They could get the kids a swing set, and maybe Oliver would build them a treehouse. Willow would enjoy it too.

"What are we going to do today, Mommy?"

"Today we'll start packing up some of the things around the apartment. The movers will be here next week, and they'll put all the boxes and furniture in their big moving truck and drive it to the house. Daddy brought some boxes home. How about you and I filling a couple of them with toys from your bedroom? That will give us a good start."

"Yay, we're moving to the country! We're moving to the country," Finn sang as he picked up his remote truck and ran for his bedroom.

Sadie was glad that Finn was so happy about the move. Willow didn't seem to mind either, which surprised her. Most ten-year-old girls wouldn't want to leave their friends or change schools. Sadie and Oliver thought Willow was being so good about it because she knew it would be helpful for her mom to leave the city. Whatever the reason, life seemed to be going great, and Sadie was happy.

Finn handed toys to her while she packed them in the boxes and ran tape across the top. Sadie had to start thinking about the drive down to the house. Oliver had suggested they rent an RV and travel at night. Sadie could lie down on the bed and try to sleep. She got nervous thinking about it, but that might be the best way. Getting from the apartment to the RV was another problem. She had to overcome those difficulties in order to make her family's life better.

I'll talk to Dr. Appleton about it during the next session. She'll tell me if she thinks it's a good plan. I can't think of any other way to get down there.

Willow walked into Finn's bedroom, looked at her mom and brother, and smiled. "We're packing?"

"Yes, we're packing. Here are some flat boxes for you to tape up and put everything in them that you won't be needing for the next week. The movers will be here on Monday."

"All right. Best news I've heard in a while. I'm ready." Willow grabbed a few boxes and left for her room.

Sadie heard her phone chime and hurried to the hallway to pick it up. "Troy, good to hear from you. We've got the moving company coming on Monday, so we just started packing today."

"That's great news, Sis. We'll be so glad to have you guys closer to us. With you all the way up in Seattle, and our lives so busy the last couple years, it didn't seem like we were getting together much."

Sadie walked into the kitchen to continue talking privately. "Oliver is going to rent an RV for us to travel in on the drive down there. I'll lie on the bed and try to get some sleep while he's driving. I think I can do this, knowing how happy I'll be afterward."

"That sounds like a great idea, and I'm sure you can do

it. I have all the confidence in the world in you, Sis. So you'll be traveling Monday night, huh? Eva and I will plan on coming over Tuesday morning and help you guys unpack all day."

"Thanks, Troy. See you then."

Sadie stood at the kitchen sink and filled a glass with cold water. She took a long drink then set the glass on the counter. Leaning in over the sink, she looked out the kitchen window at the bustling city below the high-rise apartment. The sun was shining. Colorful hanging flowerpots lined the streets, and the city looked beautiful. But then, there were the people—crowds of people everywhere.

Chapter 8

Monday morning

Sadie's eyes shot open as soon as she became conscious.

It's Monday, moving day.

The tension in her head had already started, and she had a nervous stomach. Sadie got out of bed, walked into the bathroom, and opened the medicine cabinet. There they were, her pills—the bottles of Zoloft and Klonopin, waiting for her to take that night. She had dreamed about something to do with her pills not being there in the cabinet.

Just another nightmare.

Sadie took two antacids and splashed cold water on her face. Better. She could face the day. She walked into the bedroom and said good morning to Oliver, who was just getting up and tying the belt on his robe.

"Good morning, my little redhead. This is the last day we wake up in this apartment. How are you doing? Did you sleep okay?" He put his arms around her and gave her a hug.

Sweet Oliver. He was always concerned, but Sadie was not going to spoil his day with her anxieties. He knew, and that was enough. She gave him a big kiss.

"I'll go start the coffee and make breakfast. The movers will be here at nine." Sadie hurried into the kitchen to begin their very important day. All the boxes were packed, and after breakfast, she would gather the dishes, bedding, and necessities they needed for that night. Those would go in the RV with them.

The kids were awake early and gave her a hand with breakfast. They sat down at the table and ate pancakes and scrambled eggs. Everyone seemed to have a great appetite that morning. Excitement was in the air. Soon after breakfast, Sadie heard the doorbell ring. Oliver went to answer it and let the movers in. For the next few hours, Sadie watched as her furniture was taken from the apartment piece by piece and all the boxes were removed. Each time something went out the door, she felt a moment of panic, knowing that she would be going out the door herself that evening.

It was time for one more session with Dr. Appleton. Sadie went into her office and sat down on the only chair left. She opened her laptop and connected with the doctor.

"Hello, Sadie. How are you feeling about everything that's going on today?"

"Hi, Doctor. I do admit I'm feeling somewhat nervous about actually leaving the apartment and getting into the RV. I had a dream last night that my pills were gone. Of course, I knew it was an anxiety dream. I'll wait until the appropriate time this evening and take my prescription as needed. I think I'll be okay. Oliver has been my lifeline in all of this. He'll be there to support me when it's time to get in the RV, and once we arrive, he'll help me into the house."

"How did you feel when the movers were in the apartment? Did you think they were invading your space?"

"Actually, it wasn't too bad. It might have been that I was so focused on the furniture and boxes being taken out of the apartment, and what it all meant, that I didn't feel anxious with the men in there. I stayed back from them and just watched."

"That's wonderful, Sadie. Remember, you've come a long way this last year. I've seen a lot of improvement with you beginning to overcome your phobia. I really like the fact that you're taking steps to improve your and your family's life. Keep your phone handy and give me a call if you have trouble stepping out the door. If I don't talk to you tonight, call me tomorrow morning."

Sadie smiled at the screen, loving the confidence their conversations always gave her. "I'll do that. Thank you, Dr. Appleton."

She left the office to see how her family was doing. Finn helped the moving men by carrying objects that were way too heavy for him, but that was how he was, always wanting to be big and strong like his dad. Willow munched on an apple and watched everything leave the apartment.

Where is Oliver?

"Willow, do you know where your dad is?"

"Yeah, he just got a phone call that the RV had pulled up to the apartment. You can see it out the window. He's out there now talking to the guys that delivered it, probably about how to drive it."

Sadie looked out at the street below. She could see Oliver talking to a couple of men. The RV looked smaller than she'd expected, but it was only going to be used for a one-way trip on a few hours' drive down Interstate 5. Oliver was being shown how to hitch their car to the back of it. Dizziness overcame her just watching them. She walked away from the window, needing to take her mind off of it.

"Hey, kids, let's order our favorite pizza from Sanabria's Pizzeria for our last meal in the apartment."

Finn ran around the room, slapping his hands on his side and galloping like a horse. "Yay, pizzeria, pizzeria."

Willow ran for her mom's phone. "I'll call them. I'll order extra cheese."

Sadie shook her head at her daughter and smiled. Willow would go for any excuse to use her mom's phone. It didn't take much to make her kids happy. The front door opened, and Oliver came in, clearly excited about being able to drive the RV.

"It's got everything in it, and it's just a small one. We'll see how we like it. Maybe someday, we'll get a bigger one to take on vacations." He looked quizzically at Sadie.

"You never know what life will bring us in the future." Sadie raised her eyebrows and gave her husband a curious look.

The pizza arrived, and they all sat in a circle, cross-legged on the floor as they ate. The table was gone along with everything else, and the moving van was already on the road. They were having their last dinner together in the Seattle apartment. Willow said she remembered when they lived in the country house in Oregon, but Finn had only known the high-rise. They had moved up there five years ago to be close to the hubbub of city life. Oliver was an accomplished author, and Sadie was an editor. They'd met at a book seminar twelve years ago. With technology improving over the past couple of years, they knew it was possible to work from home. They both decided that would be one more reason to move to the country.

The sun was going down, and night was upon them. Time to get on the road. Sadie opened a trash bag for the kids to throw their paper plates, napkins, and the pizza box in. They had hired someone to come in and do a final cleaning the next day. She was happy that they had already called for a cleaning company to have their country home ready for them too.

Sadie went into her bathroom, opened the medicine cabinet, and took out her recommended prescriptions for the trip that night. She popped the pills into her mouth and drank a full glass of water. She placed the remaining pills in the bottles in a zippered compartment of her purse. She walked out to her family, waiting in the living room.

"I've got an idea." Willow looked happy. "Let's all hold hands and go to each room of the house to say goodbye." Sadie noticed that her daughter's eyes were on her.

Finn jumped up and down. "Yeah, and when we get to our new house, can we hold hands and say hello to every room there?"

"The answer is yes to both of you." Sadie held her hands out, grabbed theirs, and gave them a squeeze. The Hartman family went from room to room and said goodbye to the walls of their old life. They were looking forward to saying hello to their new one.

Sadie held her phone in one hand, and with her other hand, she held tightly to her husband. They all went down the elevator together. The automatic door to the sidewalk opened, and Sadie was pleased to see the RV parked right in front. When Oliver glanced at her, she nodded that it was okay. The kids went up the steps of the RV first and loudly voiced their excitement with the stove, refrigerator, and everything inside. Oliver helped Sadie walk up the steps, and she sat down on the bed and pulled a blanket over her lap. Willow snuggled beside her and put her arm around her mom. Finn begged to ride in front with his dad. Everyone settled in, and soon they were on their way to Oregon.

Chapter 9

Tuesday

Troy tiptoed out onto the balcony and tried to sneak up quietly and surprise his wife with a cup of coffee. She was lying on a lounge chair with her eyes closed, soaking up the sunshine. When he saw her, he stopped to take it all in. Her dark silky hair was swept to the side, and the long strands danced in the slight ocean breeze. He couldn't believe eleven years had already gone by since they'd fallen in love and gotten married. He loved their life together.

"Are you trying to sneak up on me?" Eva laughed and turned her head toward him with her eyes still closed.

"Well, yeah, but with your keen sense of hearing, I guess I failed on that one." He sat down on a chair next to her and handed her the cup. He leaned in and gave her a kiss.

"I was on the phone with Oliver a few minutes ago. They arrived late last night and are just now getting up. He said that Sadie did great when they left the apartment, and she relaxed on the bed in the RV during the drive down."

"That was really a good idea of his to rent that. I'm glad

it worked out for her. We were all worried about what would happen when it was time to leave the apartment."

Troy agreed then stood. "I'll go see how Jasmine's doing with breakfast, and then I'll bring a couple plates up for us. When you're ready, we'll drive over there and give them a hand unpacking. It will be great to see them."

Troy went downstairs to check on the guests. Jasmine already had the buffet table filled, and everyone was talking, laughing, and filling their plates. He greeted them then got two plates ready to take upstairs so he and Eva could eat outside at the patio table.

After breakfast, they took the half-hour drive to Sadie and Oliver's house in the town of Elk River. It had been years since they had been there, but not much had changed. A long driveway led to a beautiful two-story Victorian that had been renovated by Sadie and Troy's parents years before. Large oak and madrone trees were everywhere. Troy remembered helping his dad plant some of them. Poles holding colorful birdhouses were scattered across the yard. He honked three times as was their custom back in the day. Finn and Willow came running out of the house, clearly anxious for big hugs from their aunt and uncle. Oliver was on the front porch, sitting in a rocker, and Troy saw Sadie's smiling face at the kitchen window.

"Uncle Troy!" Finn ran and jumped up into his arms, happy as could be. Willow took a more subtle stance and walked up to Eva first, put her arm around her, and gave her a big hug. It was great seeing everyone after such a long time.

"Finn, I asked you to quit growing last time I saw you, but you still did." Eva grinned.

"I know, I can't help it. I have growing pains in my legs, and I just keep getting bigger," Finn said.

They all went into the house and greeted each other with hugs. Then they sat around the table with coffee and doughnuts before beginning to unpack.

"Sorry to hear about your renter. So he was killed in a car accident?" Troy asked.

Oliver nodded. "Yes, a freak accident. We had only met him once, but he seemed like a nice-enough guy. It was a head-on collision with another car. He was the only one killed. The weather was bad, but other than that, no one knows how it happened. We had already given him a notice. His relatives found our contact information and got in touch with us to tell us the tragic news."

"Uncle Troy, will you play Frisbee with me outside? Sometimes, Willow plays too. She's kind of good at it." Finn stood there with a glow-in-the-dark Frisbee in his hand. "Daddy, now that we're living in the country, can we get a puppy?"

Sadie laughed at her son. "You're talking pretty fast there, Finn. Maybe you've had too much sugar. Now are you asking your uncle Troy or your dad those questions?"

"I'm asking whoever wants to listen to me." He jumped up and down, still with the Frisbee in hand.

Troy smiled at his nephew. "How about you, Willow, and I throw the Frisbee in the yard for a half an hour and then we all come back in and help unpack?"

"Yay, that's a great plan, Uncle Troy." Finn grinned and ran outside.

Troy held his hand out to Willow. "Let's go, little niece."

Chapter 10

Christmas Eve

Months had passed, and Trish and Abby were still talking about the armored car heist and killing.

"I saw William's wife, Janet, at the store the other day. That poor woman. She's lost so much weight since her husband was killed. She didn't look healthy. I asked her how the kids were, and she said they were doing the best they could and that they miss their dad. She started tearing up, so I gave her a big hug and told her again how sorry I was." Trish let out a long sigh as she finished her story for Abby.

"That's so sad. I think about him all the time. Jackson is still in a coma. I know a nurse at the hospital who's kept me informed. The prognosis doesn't look very good," Abby said as she finished closing out her day's till.

Adam had heard enough. He got up from his desk chair and walked over to his door and closed it.

Will they ever stop talking about it? I'd like to come to work just one day and not have to be reminded of the heist and William's death. If Jackson regains consciousness, will he be able to identify Gabe and Lucas?

Sometimes, he wondered if everything that had happened was worth it. He worried all the time about getting caught. His stomachaches were almost constant, and he was sure he had developed ulcers. Only three more months until the agreed-upon time that he would contact Lucas and Gabe. They would meet, divide the money, and go their separate ways.

Adam was already throwing out hints about being tired of the Oregon winters. He'd told Trish and Abby a week ago that the sideways rain and icy fog that stuck around most of the winter was giving him a huge case of the blues. He informed them that he feared he would go into a depression if he had to stick around through another winter there. He made up stories about how his cousin Charles lived in Florida and loved it. He would wait a few days then mention that his cousin was a banker and how, if he moved out there, he was sure he could get a job at the bank the cousin was in charge of. Adam made it sound like something top of mind but said he had no real plans quite yet. He would put in his notice a couple of weeks before they split the money.

It was Christmas Eve, and the bank would close early. Adam looked forward to having the next few days off. The last of the old people had withdrawn their meager amounts of cash and finally left. Adam felt depressed just looking at them. They'd worked their whole lives, and unless they were getting together with family over the holidays, they would probably drive over to one of the Indian casinos and blow it all, anyway. They had high hopes of winning a huge jackpot.

Then they would come back to their sad little backward town and wait for the next time, when they would do it all over again.

How did I end up here, anyway? After business college, this job was the only one I could get. I didn't know I would be living here almost two decades without any real progress in my life. Oh well, all that's about to change.

The women said goodbye to him as they walked out the door. "Have a good Christmas, Adam."

He held his hand up and waved. "Yeah, you too. See you both on Monday."

Adam secured the safe, set the alarms, and locked up before he went out the door. He stopped at the Mexican restaurant where he had called in a takeout order earlier. He looked forward to getting home and putting his feet up. He planned to eat his dinner while watching the news. After that, he would pack a few things and drive the hour and a half to his parents' house in Portland to spend Christmas with them.

Remembering that he hadn't checked the mail for a while, he stopped in the lobby and opened his box. After grabbing a handful of papers and envelopes, he took them upstairs to go through them.

He switched on the TV, knowing the news would start soon, and went to the kitchen to get something to drink out of the refrigerator. Adam sat down with his beer and Mexican food and relaxed. The local news hadn't mentioned anything about the heist in their half-hour segment. They rarely did anymore. Once in a while, they would say they hadn't caught the suspects or that Jackson was still in a coma, and that was about it. He finished his dinner and began to sort the mail.

Bills, bills, bills. I'm sick of seeing them. Well, it won't be much longer and money problems will be a thing of the past.

Then he saw his high school newsletter. Every year, they sent one out, letting people know when the next reunion would be and what the alumni had been doing lately. Of course, everyone with a great career would be mentioned. Sometimes, his old classmates were pictured with their families in front of beautiful, massive homes. He thumbed through the newsletter, looking to see who was the big shot that year. Adam stopped and stared. He blinked, rubbed his eyes, and blinked again. He was having a hard time believing whose picture he was looking at.

It was Lucas—Lucas Castello. His picture wasn't in there because of his great success in the world. Instead, his picture had the words In Memoriam above it.

What? How the hell could that be? Lucas can't be dead. He's holding our money.

He read on. "Sad news for McKinley High. We have recently been notified that our good friend and alumni Lucas Castello was killed in a car accident. He will be missed."

Adam jumped to his feet and hurried to the window to get more light on the article. He read it again then threw the newsletter at the wall.

Now what? Where's the damn money?

He picked up his phone and called Gabe. "Did you know about this?"

"Know about what? I thought you weren't supposed to call me for six months?"

"Dammit, Gabe. Lucas is dead. Did you know he was killed in a car accident? I just found out. It's in our high school newsletter."

Gabe was silent, and Adam heard him breathing.

Then Gabe choked on his words. "What the hell? Dead? Where's the money?"

Adam continued to pace the living room floor. He went to the kitchen and got the bottle of scotch. He needed something stronger than beer—something to burn his throat when he swallowed. "How would I know, man? The plan was, he would hide it in the house, and we would meet him there to split it up. *Where* in the house is the question?"

"Damn, when was he killed?"

Adam hadn't even thought about that. He remembered throwing the newsletter against the wall. He searched and found it on the floor next to the coffee table. He picked it up and scanned the paragraph again. The car accident was a month ago.

"Okay, here it is. Damn, it was on Thanksgiving Day. What now? Is anyone living there?"

"You're asking me? I didn't even know he was dead until you called," Gabe said.

"I've got some thinking to do. We need to get down there. I'll call you back as soon as I have a plan. Let's just hope the house is empty."

Chapter 11

Adam felt a tension headache coming on. He had to think. He had to clear his head and plan. There was no way he would know ahead of time if someone was living in the house unless he drove down there and checked it out. It was definitely the time to do it. The longer he waited, the greater the chance of something going wrong. Lucas didn't own the house. He had rented it years ago, and he'd never talked about wanting to move away. He'd once said the owners lived in Seattle.

All Adam could do was be prepared for someone to be in there and consider himself lucky if they weren't. He would make two phone calls. The first was to his mom and dad to tell them he wasn't coming for Christmas. He had to have a good excuse, so he planned to make his voice sound weak and tell them he was coming down with something, the flu maybe. He would tell them he didn't want to risk being contagious and giving them anything. That would take care of them. Then he would call Gabe and say to meet him at a motel down there and to bring his gun. The thought of killing someone at the house or keeping them hostage didn't sit well with Adam, but he had to do it if he wanted the money.

Obviously, Gabe has no problem with killing anyone. He's already shown that. Now I need to find out who owns the house.

He remembered something from a few years back. The names of property owners were public records. He used to do searches of mortgage holders' names when he wanted to send out mass mailings of offers on low-interest bank loans. He would type an address in the county public records site, and the name of the property owner would come up. He needed the physical address of where Lucas had lived in order to check it on the website. Lucas had sent him cards or something over the years. Adam walked to his desk and pulled his address book out of the drawer. Thumbing through it, he came across Lucas Castello's address. There it was—1275 Mountain View Lane, Elk River, Oregon.

He sat down on his desk chair and awakened his computer. Finding the website was easy, and he typed in the address.

Okay, there it is. The property belongs to an Oliver and Sadie Hartman. Their address is in Seattle. It tells me who to expect if someone is there, but then it could already be rented to someone else.

He decided to look up their names on social media. Maybe a picture of them would show up. He brought up a popular website and searched for Oliver Hartman.

His profile came up right away. It showed a picture of a nice-looking family sitting on the grass and surrounded by trees. They were in a park somewhere. The man and woman were maybe in their late thirties or early forties and had two young kids, a boy and a girl.

Okay, so he's a well-known author, not that I would know of him since I never read for entertainment. Besides that, it just mentioned his wife, Sadie, who was an editor, and their two children. Just one happy family who lived in Seattle.

Well, damn. Adam didn't know what to do with that information, but he would keep it in mind as he planned. Next, he would call Gabe to arrange a meetup in Elk River. If anyone was in the house, the two men would have to hold them hostage until they found the money.

He picked up his phone and tapped in Gabe's contact number.

"Yeah, so what did you come up with? What are we doing?"

"I did a little searching and found out who the owners of the house are. They live in Seattle, and their names are Oliver and Sadie Hartman. That gives us a good idea of who might be in there. But then, we have to keep in mind that the house could already be rented out to someone else. It's been a month, so who knows. I typed in their names on social media sites, and they're just an ordinary family living in Seattle. Nothing was stated like they were going to move or have moved."

"Damn, everything was going smooth. The media had stopped reporting about the heist, and now this happened. We need to get in right away. When are we doing this?"

"It's been a while since we've both been there, but remember when we were helping Lucas move in and the power wasn't on yet? We stayed at that motel along the highway. What was it called, Riverview? I'll call and reserve two adjoining rooms. Last time, we opened the room doors and partied together."

"Oh yeah, I remember the place exactly."

Adam heard something at the front door. He walked over to the window and peeked through the blinds. No one was there, then he saw the newspaper lying on the mat and realized the sound was just the bump from the paper being thrown.

I'm getting too jumpy.

He continued his conversation. "So, with Christmas, we have a long weekend. Meet me there tomorrow afternoon. We'll check into the rooms and finalize our plans. Entering the house just before daylight while people are still asleep should be the best bet. Be prepared in case there's an alarm system. I don't remember Lucas having one, but who knows if one has been installed. If there is, you'll take care of it, right?"

"Of course. That's what I do for a living, man."

"Okay, I'll reserve the rooms now in a phony name and get back to you with the room numbers."

Adam tapped the search app on his phone to find the motel's number. He made the reservation then called Gabe back and gave him the room numbers. It was time to pack, and he needed to think seriously about what he should take. After opening the hall closet, he pulled out a duffel bag then moved things around on the shelves until he found a coil of rope and a bag of large zip ties. He threw them in the bag along with a couple of bright flashlights. They might need them for searching the attic or basement or wherever the money might be hidden. That was all going to be guesswork. He threw in a change of clothes and zipped the bag.

In the bedroom, he pulled open the nightstand drawer, took out his 9 mm semiautomatic and the cleaning kit, and took them into the living room. He sat on the couch, put the kit on the coffee table, and did a thorough maintenance of his weapon while he watched TV. Adam imagined what might go down in the next couple of days. One thing he hadn't thought about was the fact that if someone was in the house, they might have already found the money. The more he thought about that, the harder he pressed down on the blue steel of his gun with the cleaning rag. Someone might have found the money and split or turned it in like a dumb bastard. The best-case scenario, it was still hidden in the house.

Did Gabe think of all that? If so, he sure didn't say anything. Now I'm even more confused about what the situation will be when we get there. Damn. The scenarios are multiplying.

Chapter 12

Christmas Day

Sadie heard the kids giggling and talking quietly. She knew it was still dark out before she even opened her eyes. It was Christmas morning, and they were probably talking about whether Santa had been there yet. She expected her two children to come bounding into the bedroom any moment and jump on the bed to wake them both up. She turned over and looked at her husband. His eyes were open, and he smiled.

"Quick, let's pretend we're asleep, and then when I squeeze your hand, we both sit up and scream Merry Christmas," Oliver told his wife.

Right on cue, Sadie heard the kids tiptoeing into their bedroom. She could tell Finn was on Oliver's side and Willow on hers. She heard them whisper.

"When do you think they'll wake up, Willow?"

"Well, it *is* still dark. Maybe we should just wake them up, anyway, since it's Christmas."

Sadie felt Oliver squeeze her hand, then they both sat up

abruptly and yelled, "Merry Christmas!"

Startled, both kids jumped then started laughing.

"Let's go! Santa probably was already here," Finn said as he ran around the bed and grabbed Willow's hand to head downstairs.

"Okay, let's get this day started," Sadie told her husband as they got out of bed and hurried down the stairs. The kids had already pulled their stockings down from the mantel and were going through them. Candy canes, chocolates, and small toys covered the coffee table. The kids knew they could eat one piece of candy right then, and they were discussing which one they would devour first. "I'll start the coffee so we can watch them with our eyes open a little more," she told Oliver as she walked toward the kitchen. She tried to calculate how much sleep they'd gotten last night after assembling two bicycles and filling the stockings. She glanced at the clock—four forty-five. Not too bad this year. They'd gotten close to five hours of sleep.

She took the coffee cups into the living room just as the kids were ready to pull the paper off the bikes. Oliver pointed the camera at them and took lots of pictures. Sadie sat on the couch and watched the festivities, happier than she had been in years. This was a good time in their lives, and moving to the country was the best thing they'd ever done as a family. She felt calmer than she had in ages and was beginning to feel like the panic attacks were a thing of the past.

"Can we ride them now?" Finn asked.

"I'll be sure to take you outside to ride your bikes soon, but we have to wait a couple of hours, at least until daylight." Oliver laughed. "Let's sit down and unwrap some of the other presents now. Willow, will you hand us each one, and we'll all watch one person at a time open them?"

"Sure, Dad." She went over and peered under the beautifully lit tree before checking the tags on the presents. "Here's one for Mom. She can go first." Willow walked proudly to her mom and handed her a small gift box.

Sadie read the label. "To Mom, from the whole family. Hmm, I can't even guess what could be in here." She shook the box slightly. Sadie untied the ribbon and peeled the paper away. She recognized the printing on the box as the name of a well-respected jewelry store. She pulled off the lid and caught her breath when she saw what was in there.

It was a beautiful heart shaped ring. Two diamonds were set diagonally on the edge of the heart, with a ruby and an emerald stone set in the center.

"Oh, it's so beautiful. I would have never dreamt of having something like this. Thank you, guys. I love it."

The kids walked over and snuggled next to her on the couch, looking at the ring.

"See, Mom, it's our birthstones. Our whole family. You and Dad's birthdays are in April, so there's two diamonds, one for each of you. My birthday is in July, so there's a ruby, and Finn's is in May, and his birthstone is an emerald."

Sadie looked up at Oliver, and her eyes pooled with tears. "I love it."

Finn ran over to the end table and grabbed a tissue for his mom. "Here you go, Mom. It's okay. Put it on your finger."

She did, and it fit perfectly. "Okay, everyone." She dabbed at her eyes. "Who's next?"

"It's Dad's turn," Willow said. She walked over and picked up a gift with her dad's name on it.

Oliver smiled at her when she gave it to him. "Well, somebody knows how to really wrap a present beautifully." He opened it and said how much he loved the analog watch that was in the box.

"Thanks, everyone. My old watch wasn't keeping correct time, so this is perfect."

"Okay, whose turn is next?" Finn asked as he jumped up and down.

"Ladies first. Remember, Finn?" his dad reminded him.

"Okay, I'll get a present for Willow. Here you go. I see your name on it."

Willow smiled at her little brother as she pulled the ribbon loose. It was a small box, just like her mom and dad's. Inside the box was a watch, but it was different from her dad's—a digital watch with a large black face on it.

"What? How does this work?" she asked.

Sadie answered, "This is a very special watch. It's kind of like a real phone. Your dad and I feel good about giving this to you because it will be strapped to your wrist, and a child of ten years old could easily lose a phone. You can text and talk on it."

"Really? That's so cool. Thank you." Willow hugged her mom and dad. "Let's try it out and call someone."

"We should wait until Finn opens his special present, and then we'll get your watch charged and ready to go," Oliver told his daughter.

Finn sat back on the couch with a smile on his face,

waiting for his turn. It was a small package, just like the ones that the rest of the family got. He tore off the paper and opened the box. It was a watch with a Mickey Mouse image on its face. "Yay, I love it. Mickey Mouse is my favorite. Thank you, Mom and Dad. We all have watches now, except Mom has a ring."

"Yes, and I really love my ring. Thanks, you guys." The Hartman family continued with their tradition of opening the presents one by one.

The morning went by fast, and Sadie realized that Troy and Eva were coming over in a couple of hours for Christmas dinner. She let her family know that she would be in the kitchen for a while.

An hour later, Willow came in and asked her mom if she would like some help. Willow demonstrated that her watch was charged and worked great and that she could call or text someone right then. Sadie let her know that she and Oliver had asked Uncle Troy to accept her smart watch calls and texts on his phone. So that part was already set up. She could text or call them and find out what time they would arrive. She let Willow know what their phone number was and told her to take it from there.

Sadie watched as her daughter figured it out. The text went through, and the answer was that they would be there within one hour.

"This is so cool. Thanks again, Mom. I love it. Plus, it has GPS on it. Look, it shows where we are right now." Willow touched a circular icon on the watch face, and a screen appeared, showing their location.

Sadie laughed. "You caught me. That's one of the main reasons your dad and I wanted you to have it. I'm so glad you like it, my sweet daughter. Now help me with this turkey."

Chapter 13

Adam pulled the Denali up close to the office door at the Riverview Motel. He walked in, made small talk with the receptionist, and paid with cash after giving a phony name. He went to his room, unlocked the adjoining door, and waited for Gabe.

An hour later, Gabe arrived. He walked into Adam's room with a couple of beers in hand. "Hey, man, it's time. Let's get this thing figured out and done."

"Yeah, before I checked in, I drove past the house that Lucas was living in. There were two cars in the driveway. Of course, it's Christmas Day, and most people have family and friends over. So that probably means that somebody is living there and has company. Or it could be that they have two vehicles of their own. Who knows? The thing is, the house is occupied. So we're going in tonight with guns and taking it from there. Waiting around and trying to figure out what's going on would just be a waste of time."

They sat at the table and tried to remember how the house was laid out.

"From what I recall the last time we were there, the easiest way to enter would be through the kitchen door. Its entrance was at the back of the house. It was a door with a window taking up half of it. Easy break-in," Gabe told him.

"You're right. We'll use a cutter and suction cup so when the glass breaks, it won't fall and make noise. Do you have those with your tools?"

"Oh yeah, I'm prepared with whatever we may need."

"We have to do this in silence. If they hear us, they'll have the heads-up to call the cops or get a gun. I remember the layout from the entry. There was a large front door that looked solid. A big staircase on the right, the living room was to the left. A bathroom was off of the hallway, and a library or room with lots of shelving was next to the kitchen. Upstairs were, what, four bedrooms and a bathroom?"

"I think so. I never understood why Lucas wanted to live in such a big house. It was only him."

Adam took a drink of his beer. "I know. I think when he decided to rent it, he was planning on marrying Renée. They broke up a few months after he was already in. He liked having a lot of space, so he continued to live there. Poor bastard, now he's dead."

"We'll miss him, but hey, more money for us."

They planned to take one vehicle over there and park close to a tree, out of sight of the road and house. Gabe had his bag of tools with him and would take care of the alarm system if there was one. They would wait for whoever was in there to wake up and come downstairs. Then, they would secure the hostages, find the money, and get out.

"Did you bring a mask?" Adam asked.

Gabe looked at him and shook his head. "No, I didn't think of it."

"Well, I'm not surprised. I brought you one." He pulled a black nylon ski mask out of his duffel bag and threw it at Gabe. "Here you go. With that on, all they can see is your eyes. I'll be wearing my glasses, so that will disguise me a little more. I've got gloves for both of us, too, so no fingerprints will be left behind. I know you've already got murder under your belt, but I'd rather get the money without killing anyone, if possible. We'll keep our masks on until we have whoever is in the house tied up and blindfolded. If they don't see us, they can't identify us."

"So you've got the rope?" Gabe asked.

"Yeah, I've got zip ties too. Easier than rope. Which gun are you packing? I've got my nine-millimeter Smith and Wesson with a clip." Adam took it out of his duffel bag and showed it to Gabe.

Gabe snickered. "You still got that thing? You've had it forever. I brought my Kimber forty-five."

"Is that what you used to kill the armored car guard?"

"Yeah, my weapon of choice."

Adam put his gun back in the duffel bag. "Okay, I think we've gone over everything. I need to get a few hours of shut-eye."

The next morning, they got into Adam's Denali and left the motel at five o'clock. They drove the fifteen minutes in silence. They'd gone over every detail, and they were ready. When they got close to the house, Adam turned off the headlights and pulled in slowly. He continued on the gravel driveway and parked behind the garage, under a tree. His

Denali couldn't be seen from the road. Before he opened the door, he flipped a switch to turn off the interior lights. The moon was full, and they could see the yard and house without getting out the flashlights. Adam had his 9 mm tucked behind his belt as well as a small backpack with zip ties, rope, and blindfolds. Everything he needed.

"Put on your mask. Let's check for any kind of security system as we head for the back door," Adam said.

Gabe grabbed his bag of tools, then they separately made their way to the house, staying close to trees for cover. Adam glanced at the windows for any interior lights that might be on. He saw that a couple of rooms were illuminated upstairs and one downstairs, probably from night-lights. His eyes followed the eaves, searching for evidence of a security system. None was found. He got to the back door first, and Gabe soon met him there.

Adam pulled a dog treat out of his pocket and watched for movement in the yard. He was prepared to quiet a pet if one was around. He kept an eye open at the windows for any change in room lights, while Gabe got to work on the door glass with the suction cup and cutter. Within five minutes, the circle was cut, and the suctioned piece of glass pulled out. Gabe reached in with a gloved hand and turned the doorknob. A night-light lit their way as they quietly entered the kitchen and continued down the hall to the living room.

Adam knew that looking around for money would be useless and make too much noise. He motioned for Gabe to sit down, relax, and wait for someone to come down the stairs. Action would happen soon enough. They just needed to wait.

Chapter 14

Adam listened, and the sound of footsteps and soft conversation was coming from upstairs. One voice sounded like a kid whining. He gripped his gun tight in his hand and looked over at Gabe to see if he'd heard it. Gabe nodded, his gun drawn. The noises soon stopped, and everything got quiet again.

The waiting game continued as Adam looked around the room. A Christmas tree was surrounded by kids' toys scattered everywhere, so a family lived there. The fireplace mantel had stockings hanging on it with their names in glitter—Oliver, Sadie, Willow, and Finn. That told him that it was definitely the Hartmans who occupied the house. He wondered who would be first to come down the stairs. He glanced at Gabe again.

Dammit, he's actually falling asleep. What happened to him these last few years? He used to be mentally with it and took things more seriously. Once the money's split up and I put in my notice at the bank, I'm out of here. I hope I never see him again.

Then he heard a door opening and footsteps coming down the stairs.

Here we go. Let the games begin.

A young girl appeared at the bottom of the stairs. Her eyes widened when she saw them. She screamed, "Dad, Dad, what are they doing here?"

Adam pointed the gun at her and waited, knowing that more people would soon arrive. He heard heavy footsteps next—Oliver.

He looked shocked as he yelled, "Get the hell out of my house! What are you doing here? What do you want?" He screamed at Adam as he pushed Willow and told her to get upstairs.

"I'll ask the questions, Oliver. You'll take the orders. Get your wife and kids down here, now."

"Like hell I will."

Next came the sound of hurried footsteps bounding down the stairs. Step one was completed. The family was all in one spot. The woman screamed at Adam.

He stood up and aimed his gun at Oliver's head. "The first things I want are your phones. Where are they?" He waited but didn't get the answer he wanted. It was time to spring Gabe on them. "My associate will gladly escort your wife upstairs to get them."

That statement resulted in the answer he wanted. Gabe went to gather phones and laptops and destroy any computers throughout the house.

The kid decided to yell at him, which surprised Adam. The little guy was brave. Adam would have to watch out for him.

"I want all of you to sit down on the couch now." Adam

waited until they had convinced each other to do as told. Gabe came back into the room. He threw two phones and a laptop on the floor and smashed them with the heel of his boots.

"Now this could be easy or devastating, it's your choice. I only have one question. Where's the money?" They played dumb, or maybe they really didn't know. Adam wasn't sure which. It would take more threats to find out. He pointed the gun at Oliver and asked again.

"If you're so sure there's money in this house, then you tell me," Oliver snarled.

That was enough. He grabbed Sadie's arm and yanked her up off the couch. Oliver started to jump to his feet but stopped when his wife pleaded with him to stay still. The kids were hysterical. Adam turned his gun away from Oliver and pressed it against Sadie's temple.

"I'm losing my patience," Adam said as he pulled Sadie closer. "Where's the money?"

"I'm telling you the truth. We know nothing about any money. We just moved here a few days ago. Don't you think I'd tell you if I knew? I'd do anything to get you guys out of here. Money doesn't matter to me. I just want to keep my family safe."

Adam believed him, but he didn't want to show weakness. Lucas would've been the type to hide the money in a safe spot where no one would accidentally come across it. It was time to secure the hostages and start tearing through the house. He glanced at Gabe, who looked like he was ready to accept whatever instruction Adam had to give.

Gabe seemed to love the drama.

"My associate will secure your family so we can search the house since you insist that you don't know where it is." Adam tossed his bag to Gabe and told him to go ahead, starting with Oliver first. "I want them separated. Tie him up to a kitchen chair and take the rest of the family upstairs." That statement got another rise out of Oliver. Adam could tell that Oliver would kill him if given the chance.

Gabe pointed his gun at Oliver and jerked his head toward the kitchen. "Move it." The kids screamed again, but their dad consoled them and said everything would be all right. As soon as they left the living room, Adam told Sadie to sit back down. She did as asked then put her arms around her children.

Adam paced the floor, waiting for Gabe to come in and secure the rest of the family and blindfold them. He couldn't wait to get his ski mask off. He could feel his sweat beading up underneath it. The family put their heads down and whimpered quietly until Gabe came back in. Then their heads lifted with looks of fear on their faces.

"Take them upstairs. I'll check on the dad to make sure he's secure and then meet you up there."

Gabe pointed his gun at Sadie. He jerked his head toward the staircase and told them to go. Sadie gathered her children in front of her, and they slowly climbed the stairs, with Gabe and his gun following close behind.

Adam walked into the kitchen to check out Oliver's bindings. His blindfold was on tight, his hands were zip-tied through the rungs of the chair, and his ankles were securely bound together with the rope. Gabe had done a decent job. Adam sat down on a kitchen chair and faced his hostage.

"Okay, it's just you and me now. Fess up and tell me where the money is. As soon as I have it, we're out of here, and you and your family will be all right. Keep stalling, and I can't tell you what my associate may do to your wife and kids. Sometimes, he's out of my control."

Oliver sobbed. His chest was sucking in and out rapidly with his heavy breathing. "Man, please believe me. I wish I knew if there was money hidden here. There's a huge basement that I haven't even gone into yet since we moved in a few days ago. There are cubbyholes and crawl spaces all over the attic. Maybe the money is hidden in one of those places."

A red ball sat on the floor, and Adam picked it up and threw it across the room. He watched Oliver's head jerk around, following the sound. Once again, Adam thought that Oliver was telling the truth. Adam pulled off his ski mask and watched to see if Oliver reacted. He didn't. The blindfold was doing its job. Adam walked over to the kitchen sink, turned on the cold water, and splashed his face.

Gabe walked in. "They're secure." He pulled off his mask. "Now what?"

Adam jerked his head toward the living room, motioning for Gabe to follow him. When they got there, Adam said he believed that the family didn't know where the money was.

"Yeah, well, I bet a few punches to the dude's face will give us some answers," Gabe said.

"Knock it off, man. I call the shots here. Throwing

punches isn't going to get us answers. Don't forget, I'm the one who had the idea to get the money in the first place. I got all the information and set up the plan. Sure, I know you guys did the physical stuff, but it would've never happened without the fact that I was working at the bank and knew the driver's schedule. Now I think we should stick together and start in the attic first. If we don't find anything there, we'll go to the basement. Let's hope we don't have to dig outside or smash in some of the walls around here. Think like Lucas. Where would he hide it?"

Chapter 15

Eva walked out of the house to find Troy. She knew he was clearing out branches that had fallen and blocked the driveway. The wind gusts had been powerful that morning.

When Troy stopped the chain saw, Eva hollered, "How are you doing? Do you need any help?"

Troy looked up at her. "Sure, you can stack those logs over by the firepit."

Carrying two logs at a time, she built up the stack and saw that Troy was finished and the driveway was clear.

"I'm glad they didn't hit any of the structures around here when they broke off. A couple of those gusts this morning must have been close to ninety miles an hour. We're pretty lucky that we just had a few large branches fall in the driveway. I think it's died down enough now that there shouldn't be anything to worry about. Coastal storms are wicked. We find that out each year." Troy took off his safety glasses and gloves.

"They sure are. But as bad as it can get, I still love living on this bluff and watching the storms come in. Oh, by the way, we just got a phone call for a private investigation case.

It was from a woman who wants to hire one of us to follow her husband. She thinks he's having an extramarital affair, and she wants to know for sure."

After Troy picked up the chain saw, they walked together to the toolshed. "Sad to say, that's about the most common type of work that we get," Troy said.

"I know. A lot of marriages don't last anymore. I'm sure ours will, though. I'm beginning to think you're a keeper." Eva smiled as she grabbed Troy's free hand.

"You sure? It's only been eleven years. Should we give it a few more decades before making an important decision like that?"

They laughed and held hands on their way to the house.

"Since it's my turn to go up to Portland to work a case, I told her I would be the one meeting with her tonight when she gets off work. I'll leave after lunch. There's probably no food at all in the refrigerator up there, so I better stop at a store and stock up for a couple of days."

"Yeah, I'm sure if there is anything in the refrigerator, it needs to be thrown out by now. It's been close to two weeks since I was up there."

"So, my appointment is at ten o'clock tomorrow morning. The client's name is Marianne Davenport, and her husband's name is Edward. I'll leave the information for you upstairs on our bedroom desk. With my Nikon camera and telephoto lens, I'm sure after a couple of stakeouts, I'll have the evidence she needs."

"Sounds good, babe. You know I'll miss you like crazy. I'll keep busy, though. The yard work here never ends, even in winter. Mother Nature doesn't give a break to those who live at the coast. I'll go back to visit Sadie and Oliver in a couple of days and see if they need help with anything. Be sure to keep your gun on you. You know how circumstances can turn on a dime in our business."

"I always do and always will." She remembered all too well some of the dangerous situations in the past. "I'll give Jasmine the list of guests who are coming in within the next few days. I'm so glad we have her to help us out. She'll handle everything. I'll go up to the house to start packing and see you at lunch."

Eva walked into the kitchen to let Jasmine know her plans. "Do I smell fresh bread? You've been busy this morning, I see."

"Yep, I love baking. I'm putting together a lasagna too. After that windstorm we had, lasagna and baked bread have been on my mind. It seems to be just that kind of a day."

"Well, it will be just you and Troy holding up the fort for a few days. I'm going up to Portland to work on a case. I'll make a copy of this week's reservations for you so you know who's coming and going."

The timer went off, and Jasmine opened the oven door and checked on the bread. "All right, it's perfectly browned on the top. So, you're going up to Portland? Everything will be fine here. You know we'll miss you, though."

Eva put her arm around Jasmine and gave her a squeeze. Although they weren't related, she cared for Jasmine as much as she did for her own sisters.

"I'll go upstairs, pack a suitcase, and leave right after

lunch," Eva told her, then she went up to the bedroom, opened the closet door, and stood in front of the safe. After she clicked in the combination, she opened its heavy door and took her Glock 27 from one of the shelves. She kept a pistol there at the coast and one at their apartment in Portland. She always traveled with one in her car, under the seat. She grabbed a box of ammo and a clip and laid them on her bed along with the pistol. Her briefcase contained the information on the Davenport case, and she made sure she put a copy for Troy on the desk. Her camera bag was always packed and ready.

After throwing a few shirts, a couple of pairs of pants, underwear, and pajamas into a suitcase, she was almost finished. Eva walked into the bathroom and filled a cosmetic bag. Done. Eva had the packing routine down pretty good. She and Troy had agreed to take turns going up to Portland when they worked a new PI case. She was ready for some excitement and glad it was her turn.

The wonderful smell of lasagna and fresh bread wafted up the stairs. It was time to eat lunch, say her goodbyes, and get on the road.

Chapter 16

On the way up to the attic, Adam decided to check on Sadie and the kids. Gabe said he had secured them in the girl's room. When Adam opened the bedroom door, all three of them were sitting on the bed. Sadie stiffened her shoulders and scooted back protectively toward her children. The boy began to cry.

"What do you want with us? These kids do not need to go through this. You're a terrible person. There's no reason to keep us tied up when you can just barricade the door and go about your business."

Adam stood there and looked at them. "That might be in the plans. But for now, let's see how well you and the kids behave the way you are." To make sure their blindfolds were on tight, he rapidly moved his arm to see if they flinched. He walked toward them to check the zip ties securing their wrists, and the ropes around their ankles. Everything was tight. They weren't going anywhere.

After leaving the bedroom, he continued down the hall and climbed the stairs to the attic. Gabe was already up there throwing things around and making a bunch of noise.

"Hey, can you quiet down? We can search without waking the whole neighborhood, you know."

Gable rifled through boxes and tossed them to the side. "There's no one around for miles. What are you talking about?"

"We don't know if there's anyone living close. There could be a house beyond those trees in the backyard. I'm just saying you need to stop making unnecessary loud noises," Adam said.

Adam began his search from the front corner of the attic, looking up into rafters and behind old furniture. He noticed that plywood had been tacked up on some of the walls but not all of them. A crowbar lay on top of a toolbox, so he used it to pull the plywood off and get a close look at what was behind it.

Gabe yelled, "What the hell, man! There're rats up here, dammit. One just ran over my boot." He picked up a metal box and threw it at the rat, missing it by a couple of feet. The rat made its way into a small hole in the wall.

Adam shook his head and continued his search using the crowbar to pull off plywood. "Attics and basements are their homes. Just ignore them. They're not going to hurt you. Oliver said there was a lot of cubbyholes up here. Search everywhere and be sure you don't miss anything."

As Adam looked at the floorboard, he wondered about that area too. He walked slowly across the attic, looking down to see whether any of the planks had been loosened recently. Lucas wouldn't have haphazardly thrown that kind of money in a cardboard box. It had to be inside the wall, floor, or up against the ceiling somehow. They had a lot of attic to cover and continued searching for the next two hours. Every corner was checked, and all the boxes had been searched.

Adam put down the crowbar. "I think we can call it quits up here. Let's look in on the family and head to the basement."

Back in the bedroom, they saw that Sadie and the kids hadn't moved at all. Gabe continued on to check on Oliver. Adam closed the bedroom door and stood with his ear against it for a minute to listen. The whimpering continued with Sadie assuring the kids that everything would be okay. He went into the kitchen, and Gabe leaned against the refrigerator, chomping down on a turkey drumstick. Oliver was still in the chair, bound and secure.

"What the hell are you doing? This is no time to stuff your face. Get to work," Adam told Gabe.

His friend took another bite, threw the bone in the sink, and left the room.

Oliver lifted his head. "Is my family okay? Did you find your damn money?"

"Now Oliver, don't you think I'd tell you if we found it? We'd be out of here right away. Believe me, we're not staying any longer than we have to. And your family is just fine."

"What makes you think there's money hidden here, anyway?"

Adam leaned against the counter. "Think about it. The less you know, the better off you are. All I can say is when we find it, we're out of here. We'll be very happy to leave."

Adam made his way into the basement. Gabe was taking boxes down from a large metal shelving unit and rifling through them.

"What is it with you and the boxes? I told you, Lucas would've been smarter than that. The money is probably hidden within a part of the house itself."

Gabe kicked a big box over toward the wall. "Look around. Sure, there's a dirt floor here, but it's packed down hard. I already walked all over it. I don't see any breach in the floor that looks like it could have happened within the last couple of months."

Adam agreed as he checked for himself. The dirt was so hard from years of being packed down that it almost looked like cement. He glanced at the ceiling as he walked around the basement. It was filled with a maze of pipes. Then he took a close check of the walls for a hidden compartment. Nothing looked like a possible spot for hiding two large bags. He was discouraged.

"Finish checking through the boxes. I'll start searching each room in the house for a wall that looks like it may have been replaced or tampered with recently. I'll check inside heating vents and anything else I can think of. If you want to take a break from down here, go outside to the garage to see if you can find a shovel. This time of year, there won't be a garden, so look for an area of dirt that looks like it has been dug up recently. He may have buried the money in the backyard."

Gabe agreed. They left the basement and went upstairs to the living room. Gabe grabbed his jacket and said he would go outside through the kitchen door and check on Oliver on his way out.

I might as well start in this room and work my way through the house. Adam stood there trying to think like Lucas would have. He looked at the floor and reminded himself to check for loose floorboards. Walking slowly past each wall, he watched for signs of new Sheetrock, fresh paint, or something that appeared unusual. Wainscoting had been installed halfway up the wall. Something could be hidden behind it. He checked all the nails that held up the wainscoting panels to see if any of them looked like they had recently been nailed back in. Adam moved furniture away from the walls to check behind them and the floorboards underneath. Nothing seemed suspicious. He cleared the living room and went on to another area of the house.

The office close to the kitchen would be the next room he checked. A massive bookcase took up a whole wall. Statues, vases, and knickknacks, as well as a variety of books, were scattered across the shelves. Adam decided to check the floors and perimeter of the room first and save the shelves for later. He pushed the desk back and inspected the floor underneath and all around it. He continued on to the other walls in the room, seeing nothing out of the ordinary. He took a step back and stared at the bookcase. He looked for an oversized gap between the shelf joints—or a sign of a secret door or anything that looked unusual.

Adam hung his head and closed his eyes. He felt a headache coming on. He brought his hands up to his temples and rubbed them to relieve the tension. They needed to find the money and fast. It was already two o'clock in the afternoon. The longer this went on, the worse things could get. *That,* he knew. When he opened his eyes, he focused on the lowest shelf, close to the floor. The wood was chipped on the bottom board. The dark mahogany finish was scraped off on a couple of inches on both sides of a shelf joint. Adam walked over, kneeled, and studied it. Something had happened to two of those boards recently, and the wood had been cut. He set aside a ceramic statue of a bird. He put his hand up against the back wall of the shelf and pressed. There it was—the wall opened. A spring had been attached. He pulled out the shelving around it.

This is it. This is where Lucas hid the money. I can see the bags.

He almost reached in and pulled them out but decided the smart thing would be to tell Gabe. That way, they could retrieve and count the money together. Adam wanted to get his half and go on his way. He stood up and walked to the kitchen. Oliver was in the same position that he'd been in before. He raised his head but didn't say anything. Adam walked out toward the garage and found Gabe digging a hole behind it.

"Hey, you can put the shovel down. I found it."

"You did? Where was it?" Gabe threw the shovel to the side and walked toward Adam.

"Believe it or not, Lucas made a hidden compartment in the bookshelf. It had a spring-loaded opening. I saw the bags and left them there so we can both go in, count it together, and get the hell out of here."

Gabe hurried toward the back door. "Let's do it, man."

As they entered the kitchen and walked past Oliver, he asked for a drink of water. "Soon enough, Oliver. Soon enough." Adam continued toward the office. He kneeled down in front of the opening along with Gabe and pulled out the first bag, then he reached in deeper and got a tight hold on the straps of the next one and pulled it to him. Gabe was already opening the first bag.

"All right, we've talked about this for years, and the money is right here in our hands. We did it." Gabe scooped the bundles of money in both hands and tossed them in the air.

Adam began to stack them in equal heights. "Seven hundred thousand dollars each. I can do a lot with that. Okay, so we have one-hundred-dollar bills banded in stacks of ten thousand dollars. Let's count out seventy stacks, twice. The smaller denomination bundles we don't care about right now."

They sat next to each other on the floor and counted. When the two stacks were of equal height, they stuffed them in the bags.

"Let's go. We got what we came here for." Gabe tightened the straps on his bag.

"Wait, one more thing. We've got to take the woman with us."

Gabe stood up and looked at Adam like he was crazy. "Why the hell would we do that? We don't need her. Are you losing it, man?"

"Look, we have them tied up so tight, who knows when they'll get loose. I don't feel good about kids dying from thirst, or anyone for that matter. We can't let them go because the cops would be after us right away. If we take the woman with us, tied like she is and blindfolded, we can drop her off somewhere after dark. She couldn't identify us, since she won't see the type of vehicle we have or our license plate. We wore gloves all the time we were in the house, and they never saw our faces. We'll cut the zip ties, take off her blindfold, then dump her in the country somewhere. She'll still be alive. It'll take her a while, but sooner or later, she'll get to a phone, call the cops, and the family will be rescued."

Gabe picked up the second bag. "Whatever. You're nuts, man. I don't have anything to lose since I've already killed someone. I'm putting these in the Denali. Do whatever you need to do and let's go."

Chapter 17

"Mommy, what are we going to do? Are the bad guys going to hurt us? Are they going to kill Daddy?" Finn asked between sobs.

Sadie put her cheek against the top of Finn's head and rested it there. "Everything will be fine, sweetheart. They'll leave as soon as they find their money. We'll be okay. Don't you worry."

Willow slid her body as close to her mom as she could and said, "My shoulders and arms hurt, Mom. Do you think they'll cut the ties on our wrists soon? My arms are getting numb."

Sadie felt a rush of tears welling up in her eyes. Her blindfold caught them before they could roll down her cheeks.

How can two people be so cruel as to tie up and blindfold children like this? What kind of threat can two young kids be? I hope both men burn in hell.

She had to keep her voice strong to show the kids that she had the courage and confidence that everything would be okay. Since they hadn't seen the men's faces, chances were good that they would be all right. She was glad the men had masks on.

"I'm sorry, Willow. Can you flex your fingers and try to get the numbness out of your arms?"

Willow told her mom she would try but said her fingers were beginning to get numb too. She could hardly feel them. Sadie decided that when one of the men came back, she would plead with him to cut the kids' wrist ties. Finn was crying again, his little body shaking as he sat next to Sadie.

"Mom, when did Uncle Troy say he was coming back over? Was it today or tomorrow? He said that he would see us soon, just before he and Aunt Eva left last night," Willow said.

A shock wave traveled through Sadie's body. She had forgotten about that. Troy did say he was coming back to see if he could help with the rest of the unpacking. She thought he said it would be tomorrow, or the next day, not today. She didn't want to disappoint Willow by telling her.

Willow suddenly spoke up with excitement in her voice. "Mom, last night while I was falling asleep, I was looking at my watch. It's somewhere in this bed. I took it off my wrist so I could use it with both hands. Uncle Troy's phone number is in it. We can't see it because of the blindfolds, but we can feel for it and try to remember where the digital buttons were on its face."

Sadie couldn't believe what she was hearing. She almost screamed with joy as she tried to remember the options on the watch. "Let's move around and try to find it. It's hard with our hands behind us, but if you fell asleep with it in bed, it has to be somewhere tucked in the blankets or under the pillow. Let's feel around for it right where we're sitting.

All three of them did just that. They sat still, and although their wrists were bound, they moved their hands around the best they could. No one found the watch.

"Kids, we have to do this methodically, starting at the head of the bed. Let's all try to stand up and move close to the pillow. Then we'll sit down and feel for it again."

Although their ankles were bound with ropes, they stood up and shuffled toward the head of the bed. Sadie knew that the watch would most likely be by the pillow since that was where Willow was looking at it while she fell asleep. They sat back down and moved their fingers around to try to find it. Then Sadie felt it. The edge of the watchband was close to the pillow. "Kids, I've got it." She wiggled her fingers, trying to grab it with her fingernails. Her heart sank as it moved from her side closer to the edge of the bed. Then she heard a soft thump as it dropped to the floor.

"Oh no, it fell," Finn said.

"Don't worry, Finn. I'll roll over to that side of the bed and bend down to pick it up. I'm just so glad that Willow thought of it. I forgot all about it. We'll be okay now."

"Mom let me do it. I think I can get it easier than you since I'm smaller," Willow said.

Sadie listened as her daughter lay down on the bed and rolled to the other side. She heard Willow put her feet on the floor then get to her knees. The watch had to be just inches from where she was kneeling.

"Mom, my blindfold shifted when I rolled over. I can see

straight down a little bit with my right eye. There it is, I've got it! We can call Uncle Troy."

"Thank God, Willow. I know there's no way of calling 911 or anyone who isn't programmed into your phone, but we can tell him to call the cops. Sit up on the bed and push it toward me. Keep your eye on the watch and tell me if I'm pressing the right buttons."

Willow sat down on the bed with her back to her mom, holding the watch in her fingertips. Sadie scooted over until her back was close to Willow's and felt for it. Touching the face of the watch, she was overjoyed.

"Okay, turn your head so you can see the watch through the opening in your blindfold. Now, I'll touch different parts of it as you're watching me. Tell me if I'm moving my fingers in the right way."

"Go ahead, Mom. Touch your thumb to the bottom left of the watch face. No, that's the GPS symbol. Touch the other end of the watch. Now press. You got it, Mom. Now swipe your thumb to the left. No, the other way, toward the pillow. Good. Now I see the round *call* icon for Uncle Troy's phone."

It slipped out of Sadie's fingers right after she pressed the call symbol. They heard footsteps on the stairs, getting louder as they neared the landing. Troy's phone was ringing. "Hi, I'm sorry I missed your call. Please leave a message, and I'll get back to you as soon as possible."

Oh my God, it's his voicemail. Sadie tried to turn her body to talk into the watch.

"I've got it, Mom. I'm closer." Willow put her mouth near

the phone and spoke in a quiet voice. "Uncle Troy, there are bad guys here. Help us. Hurry." She had the foresight to touch the mute button after completing her message.

"Willow, quick, pick it up and put it in my pocket."

Miraculously, Willow was able to grab the watch and drop it in her mom's robe pocket, just before the door opened.

Chapter 18

Troy decided to torch the burn pile. The wind had completely died down, and the air was cold and crisp. It was the perfect time. Troy lit the bottom of the pile and stood back as the flames rose. They began to consume the twigs and small branches that the storm had brought down. Cypress trees growing next to the driveway were beautiful but always took the brunt of the damage in the windstorms. He grinned while thinking how fun it would be to toast marshmallows on a stick when the flames died down and the coals were glowing. Eva would've loved that. She had probably arrived in Portland by then. Maybe he should call up to the house and ask Jasmine if she would like to bring some marshmallows down. A couple of hot dogs would be good, too, and they could call it dinner. Troy reached in his pocket to pull out his phone.

He saw that he had a voice message from Willow's smart watch. That was such a great gift for a ten-year-old. She wasn't quite old enough for a phone, but the watch would enable her to keep in touch with her parents. He clicked on the voice message.

"Uncle Troy, there are bad guys here. Help us. Hurry."

What the hell? What is she saying? That's not something to kid around about. Willow is old enough to know that.

Troy grabbed a stick and poked the burning branches. The message seemed too real to be a prank. Willow's voice sounded urgent. He wouldn't relax until he went over to his sister's house. If he called back and the danger was real, whoever the *bad guys* were would hear the ring. He had to leave. Troy scrolled through his phone contacts until he got to Jasmine's number.

"Cypress Bluff Bed-and-Breakfast, Jasmine speaking."

"Jasmine, I'm down at the burn pile. I have to leave right now. Something may be wrong at Sadie's house. Please come down and watch the fire for me. There's a water hose lying next to it." Troy headed for his Jeep. If the message was serious, time was of the utmost importance.

"Of course, Troy, go."

He wondered where his gun was located, then he remembered it was under the Jeep's seat. He hadn't put it back in the safe after his last case. He slapped his hand against his hip to make sure he felt the keys in his pocket. Picking up his pace, he ran up the driveway. Within five minutes, he was close to his Jeep. He pulled out the key fob and unlocked it while he was still running. Troy got in, started the engine, and peeled out, going down the bluff road at a rapid speed. It usually took half an hour to get to their house from his, but he thought he could do it safely in less than twenty minutes. The road was full of curves and turns. Troy used his knowledge of brake and release to get the best driving time.

My God, that family has been through enough with Sadie's panic attacks, our dad dying from the virus, and then the move down here. I hope that this is a prank of some kind.

Troy knew the smart thing to do would be to have the cops meet him out there. If it was a prank, though, he would never live it down. He didn't care—better safe than sorry. When he got to a straight stretch of road, he could make a quick call. He pulled to the side of the road, took the phone out of his pocket and tapped the contact for one of his best friends since childhood, State Trooper Michael Stevens. He wasn't sure Mike would be on duty the day after Christmas, but there was a good chance he would be. He was single, and his job was his life. He'd recently moved up in rank from an officer working for the county to serving the whole state of Oregon. Mike picked up on the second ring.

"Hey, Troy, how was your Christmas?"

"Mike, remember I told you my sister and her family were moving back down here and living in the house Sadie and I grew up in?"

"Yeah, you said you were worried about your sister during the move because of her panic attacks and agoraphobia. What's up?"

"Well, I'd like you to meet me over there now if you can. My ten-year-old niece got one of those smart watches for a present, and ten minutes ago, I heard a voice message from her that she sent earlier stating that bad guys were there and for me to help."

"Yeah, I can head over there. Are you sure it's not a joke of some kind?"

"My gut feeling says no. She's a responsible kid. I'm on my way to the house now. I'll be there in twenty minutes. Do you remember where it's at? It's been years since you've been there."

"I remember, and it's slow here. I'll get someone for backup and see you there in close to half an hour."

Troy was glad he'd made the call. Mike had helped him out on numerous occasions. As a private investigator, Troy could legally do only so much. A few times, though, he had ignored the legal concerns when time was of the essence and someone's life was in danger. He glanced at his phone to see if another text message had come in from Willow. There was no new text. Troy remembered his and Eva's promise to each other. They'd said they would always leave a message about where they were going if they thought they might be in a dangerous situation. He would never hear the end of it if he didn't. Looking down at his phone, he touched Eva's contact. It wasn't going through. Then he remembered he was in a dead spot and there was no cell service for a couple of miles. He put the phone back in his jacket pocket.

Realizing he was almost there, he concentrated on what to do when he arrived. He would be there before Mike, and he didn't feel like waiting for him. To brazenly drive up to the house was not the best idea in case the message was true. His sister's driveway was coming up on the left. Troy slowed down as he went by to take a look at the property. The only vehicle he could see was Sadie and Oliver's car, which was in front of the garage. Troy pulled over to the side of the road and parked. He reached under the seat, pulled out his gun, and tucked it behind his belt. He got out of the Jeep, closed the door quietly, and listened. Besides a few birds singing, he heard no sounds at all. Troy walked slowly on the driveway, hearing the crunch of gravel beneath his feet. Staying close to the trees for cover, he scanned each window, watching for any movement, as he made his way toward the front door.

He heard a scream that sounded like Sadie. Then he heard people yelling from inside the house. Troy ran for the front door with his gun ready. When he entered the house, he heard a commotion coming from the kitchen. He ran to it just in time to see a man with a tight grip around Sadie's waist and a gun to her head. They were leaving from the back door.

"Stop! Let her go now, or I'll shoot," Troy yelled.

The man turned toward him, a surprised look on his face. Then he pointed his gun at Troy and fired. The force of the bullet slammed into Troy's shoulder and caused him to fall back and hit the kitchen wall. Troy took a deep breath and pushed himself forward to hurry after the guy. He would have to think about the pain later. The guy was getting away with his sister. Troy rushed out the back door, stumbled on the steps, and fell to the ground. He was outside just in time to see the man heading to the back of the garage with Sadie still in his hold. The man turned his gun at him again and fired, but Troy rolled to his side to avoid the shot. He lay on the ground and watched as the man opened the back door of a vehicle and pushed Sadie inside. She was blindfolded, and her hands were tied. When the guy opened the vehicle's passenger-side door to get in, Troy had a clear shot. He aimed carefully and got off three shots. The man flinched and fell into the front seat. The car door closed as the vehicle peeled out down the driveway, spraying gravel.

Troy felt the burn in his shoulder getting worse. Rolling to a sitting position, he thought about what had just happened. Sadie had to be okay. He had to get to her. He grabbed his phone out of his pocket to call Mike and tell him to watch for a dark SUV that might be heading his way. He'd had no time to get a plate number on it, but if the men turned right on the road, there was a good chance that Mike would pass them on his way there. He quickly pressed Mike's contact and waited. It went right to voicemail.

Damn. They're in the dead zone. No cell service. That tells me that they'll be here within fifteen minutes. I've got to find the kids and free Oliver.

Troy knew Oliver was in the kitchen, tied to a chair and blindfolded. He'd seen him as he was running out the back door, trying to rescue Sadie. Troy tried to stand, using his right hand to grasp the handrail next to the steps and pull himself up. His left shoulder had taken the bullet. The good thing was that it was only grazed. It was the same shoulder that took a bullet a year ago when he was on the hunt to rescue Jasmine. He staggered into the kitchen, took a look at Oliver, and pulled off his brother-in-law's blindfold.

"Troy, thank God it's you. I had no idea who was here. They took Sadie. Hurry, we've got to get her back. They dragged her outside, and you know she must have panicked. The kids—we've got to find them." Then he pointed at the blood running down Troy's shoulder. "You've been shot. Are you all right?"

Troy rummaged through a kitchen drawer to find a knife or scissors to cut the zip ties. "I'll be okay. It's not the first time. I'll tie it off with a dish towel. The cops are on their way. Do you know where the kids are?" Troy found a large pair of scissors and cut the zip ties around Oliver's wrists. Then he pulled off the ropes that bound his brother-in-law's legs.

"I'm not sure. They must be somewhere in the house. I don't think they took them anywhere, just Sadie."

Troy went to the sink, filled a glass with water for Oliver, and told him to drink it and stand up slowly. He did, and then he told Troy to check upstairs for the kids.

"Hurry, I'll head that way. My legs are numb. I can't move very fast."

Troy took the stairs two at a time, yelling for them. "Willow, Finn, where are you?" He heard a scream and then sobbing that sounded like Willow. Then he heard Finn.

"Uncle Troy, is that you? Help us. Help! We're tied up in Willow's bedroom."

"Finn, Willow, I'm here." He opened the door and ran to them. The kids sobbed, and Willow was screaming for her mom and dad. It broke Troy's heart to see them tied up and blindfolded.

What kind of animals did this? He quickly took off their blindfolds and used the scissors still in his hand to cut their zip ties and free their legs. He hugged them tightly.

Finn wiped the tears from his eyes as he said, "They took Mommy away. You know she can't be outside. They took her and said she had to go with them in the car. Are they going to hurt her? Where's Dad?"

"Your dad's right behind me. He's coming upstairs, the cops are on their way, and we will find your mom."

Oliver entered the room, sobbing as he put his arms around both children and hugged them. "I'm so sorry this happened to you kids. We'll find, Mom. Don't worry. Did they hurt you at all? Are you both all right?"

"I'm just numb. I'll be better as soon as I move around," Willow said. "Other than tying us up, they didn't hurt us."

Little Finn was crying, "I want Mommy."

"Okay, we have to get some information to tell the cops," Troy said. "Do you know why they were here? Why did they break in and tie you guys up?"

Oliver told him all that he knew. "They must have broken in just before daylight. Some kind of noise woke Finn before six in the morning. At daylight, I heard Willow get up. She let out a scream when she got downstairs. That's when I ran down and saw two men sitting on the couch. The tall one had his gun pointed at her. They were wearing ski masks, and the only way to tell them apart was that one was tall and wore glasses and one was short and overweight. Sadie and Finn ran down the steps after I did. The men destroyed our phones and laptop, so we couldn't get a call out. The next thing I know, they were screaming at us, asking, 'Where's the money? Where's the one million four hundred thousand dollars?' Of course, if I'd known what they were talking about, I would've told them. I have no idea what money they were referring to. I'm pretty sure they found it, though. They had searched the house for hours, and then suddenly their whole demeanor changed, and they grabbed Sadie and left."

"The cops are here," Troy said when he heard footsteps on the stairs. "We've got to get Sadie back."

Chapter 19

The screams wouldn't stop, Adam didn't know who was yelling louder, Sadie or Gabe. He'd had enough. "Shut up, both of you. Gabe, how bad is it? Where did he get you?"

"The bullet's in my chest. He got me in the chest and my thigh. Oh my God, it hurts." Gabe held his palm against his torso. His head was bent, and his breath was coming loud and fast.

Adam already knew the answer to the question he was about to ask. "Do you want me to take you to the hospital?"

"No, I'll take my chances. I don't want to spend the rest of my life in prison."

Sadie wouldn't stop yelling, "Who did you shoot? Did you shoot my husband? Let me go, you bastards. You got your money. What do you want with me?"

"I'll tell you one thing, you bitch. If you don't shut your mouth, I'll pull over and gag you. Or just kill you and throw you out of the car, I haven't made up my mind yet. I could just shoot you right where you're lying right on the floor. There's so much blood in this car it's not going to make any difference, anyway. Now just shut the hell up!"

Adam was furious. When they'd found the money, the plan seemed to be going great—foolproof, even. Now he had a friend dying next to him and a screaming hostage on the floor in the back. Blood was everywhere. It would take some careful planning to cover that up.

He couldn't drop Gabe off at the motel to get his truck. There was no way Gabe would be able to drive. He'd be contacted sooner or later because of the plate number. Gabe would just have to say he didn't know it was stolen because he was out of town. Adam gave him a sideways glance and realized that it was only a matter of time until he was gone. It was a waste of time to wonder about an excuse for his truck. He'd have to find an out-of-the-way place to dump both bodies. Then a thought came to mind.

I should just drive to his cabin. Nobody's ever there except for Gabe. I could dump both bodies in the lake, clean the blood out of my car, and make sure there's no evidence left behind.

Adam felt better once he had another plan. It would work, and the bonus was that all the money would be his. He tried to wrap his head around that thought. Because of everything that had happened, he soon would have almost a million and a half. All he had to do was get rid of all the evidence, go back to his apartment and his job at the bank for a couple of weeks, and he was done. Done with it all. Then he would really start to live. He'd go to some other country or an island, anywhere away from that backward neck of the woods.

There was so much blood. It pooled on the floor, thick and red. Adam felt sick to his stomach. He looked away and concentrated on the road. It would be another couple of hours, at least, until he arrived at the cabin. Gabe's breath was becoming shallow. Each time Adam heard him inhale, the sound was quieter.

Who was that guy that shot him? How did he know to go there with a gun and that all this was going down? Did Gabe kill him?

Adam knew that even if the guy lived, there was no way he could identify them. They were too far away from each other for facial recognition. Adam had parked behind the garage, and the way he spun out of there, the guy couldn't have had a direct sight line to his plate number.

"When will you let me go? When you took me away from my kids, you said you would only keep me for a little while longer."

Oh my God, why didn't I gag her before I started driving?

"Shut up. I told you before, the more you babble on, the angrier I'm going to get. So stop talking and be glad you're still alive."

Gabe's body jerked. A gurgling sound came from his throat. Adam glanced over at him and saw the terror on his face. He reached toward Adam, then he suddenly dropped to the seat. His body became quiet, and his eyes were open.

Feeling nauseated, Adam had to stop to throw up. He glanced in his rearview mirror to make sure no one was behind him. He was in the country and could see the road for miles. He slowed down, pulled over, and got out just in time to heave. It felt like his guts would come up and lodge in his throat. His hands shook, and he felt dehydrated. He remembered that he always kept water in the side compartment in the back. After opening the hatch, he grabbed a bottle and took a long drink. Adam poured the rest of the liquid over his head, trying to relieve the same tension headache that he was beginning to feel on a daily basis. After pulling a handkerchief out of his jacket pocket, he shook the water from his head and dried his face. He took another bottle of water for the drive and began to walk to the front of the car.

Looking around, he saw a ditch close by. If he let her out now, it would just be a matter of time before someone found her and she told the cops everything she knew. He hadn't killed anyone yet and hoped his plan would proceed without having to do so. If she was dead, there was a good chance he could get away with everything. Adam had to decide whether to dump her there in the country—alive, as he'd originally planned—or take her to the cabin and let the lake claim her life.

Chapter 20

Marianne Davenport was the curator at a high-end art gallery in Portland. Eva read through the information in the file. Marianne and her husband, Edward, had been married for twenty-five years. He was a real estate broker and doing very well financially. He dealt with the most expensive homes and land contracts in the Portland area. He also had access to any home that he wanted to take his newest mistress to, according to Marianne. She was sick of it and wanted to divorce him. She just needed evidence of his infidelity so she could get the best possible financial settlement.

Eva sat at her desk in the Portland private investigation office, waiting for her client to arrive for their five thirty appointment. Marianne wasn't late, and at five thirty on the dot, the door opened, and a very well-dressed, perfectly put-together woman walked in.

Eva stood and offered her hand. "Hello, Mrs. Davenport. It's so nice to meet you. I'm Eva Winters."

"Hello, Mrs. Winters. I'm happy to meet you too. Your business has been highly recommended." She extended her hand for the handshake.

"Please, take a seat. May I get you some water, coffee, or tea?"

"Thank you, but I'm fine. This should be a cut-and-dried case for you. My husband's latest fling is a woman named Roxie Myers, a real estate agent. I've watched them at get-togethers for the last three months, and it's obvious they're having an affair. I have driven by houses that I know my husband is contractually involved in. Her car is always parked there along with his. I know the business enough to realize that she doesn't need to be there at that time. To be frank and to the point, I just need you to get pictures of their affair. I'll give them to my lawyer, and we'll have evidence for my day in court. My goal is to divorce him as soon as possible and get as much money in the settlement as I can."

"If it's that obvious, I'm sure I can get evidence for you right away."

She laid a large manila envelope on Eva's desk. "For visual identification, I've included enlargements of photos of my husband and business photos of this Roxie Myers woman. I've taken those from her business websites. Also, inside is a list of the current properties that he's selling. He's already called and left a message on my voicemail to say that he'll be home late and not to wait dinner for him. He said he has property research to do at the home of one of his clients, the Taylors. I already know that they're out of town. Mrs. Taylor is a patron of my gallery and has asked me to hold off on the delivery of a piece that she purchased recently. As their broker, he has the keys to their house. My gut instinct is that he's meeting that woman there tonight."

"So the address of the property that you would like me to watch tonight is in this envelope?"

Marianne took a deep breath and sighed. "Yes, and the plate number of my husband's Mercedes. I know she drives a blue SUV of some kind. That's it. I have a feeling you'll get the evidence right away. There's no love lost between us. I just want to divorce him in the most profitable way I can after his years of infidelity."

"If I'm successful in getting all that you need tonight, would you like me to email the photographs to you right away?"

Marianne pushed her chair back and stood. "Yes, you've got all my contact information. Please let me know as soon as possible. It was nice to meet you, Mrs. Winters."

After Mrs. Davenport left, Eva went upstairs to the apartment and made a sandwich to take with her on the stakeout. She opened the lunch bag and put in an apple, chips, and a bottle of water, knowing it might be a long night. Things could go quickly, and stakeouts were unpredictable. Mrs. Davenport had done most of the work for her, and it would be an easy case.

Eva's equipment consisted of her Nikon camera, long telephoto lens, cell phone, and Glock. Everything was ready and sat next to the front door. After filling her thermos with a freshly brewed pot of coffee, she was ready to go.

She typed the address of the Cedar Hills residence into her GPS and drove away. It was still daylight, and Eva wanted to get there to see the home, and hopefully the vehicles, before dark.

While she drove, she listened to music on the radio and thought about Troy. He was going to start a burn pile that day, and she hoped he would be careful. Her sweet husband was so accident-prone. She was glad she had asked Jasmine to check on him while she was gone, to make sure he was okay with the chain saw work and climbing ladders and everything else. Eva always thought that kind of work was even more dangerous than private investigations. Not necessarily for everyone, but for her husband, who seemed to have revolving-door status at the local emergency room.

She turned off the freeway and began to drive up the hill to the property. Beautiful mansions sat at the end of long driveways. Some of them had elaborate wrought iron gates. She hoped that the residence she would be watching wasn't gated. Gates had been known to cause problems with stakeouts in the past.

A ten-minute drive up the road along a lush rolling hillside and her GPS told her that she had arrived.

Perfect, no gate, and I can see the front of this gorgeous mansion from this side of the road.

He'll get a nice commission when he sells this.

Sometimes, life was just easy. Everything went smoothly without any problems. She drove on past the driveway and pulled over on the side of the road opposite the residence. She loved stakeouts that were at the top of a hill. There was at least an eighty percent chance that any vehicles would be coming up the hill and going back down the same way. She could pull on past the driveway and watch for people to come and go through her side and rearview mirrors.

She poured a cup of hot coffee from her thermos, sat back, and kept an eye on her mirrors while sipping it. It was a short wait. Twenty minutes in, Mr. Davenport's Mercedes appeared. He had his left signal on as he pulled into the driveway. Just to be sure, Eva compared the plate number to the information from Mrs. Davenport's paperwork. As he parked and got out, she snapped a couple of photos. Instead of going up to the door, he leaned against the front of his car and folded his arms against his chest.

Eva changed the lens to her longest telephoto. Looking through the camera for a closer view, she got off a few more shots. She noticed his eyes were closed while he stood there. Then she watched as he opened his eyes, took the phone out of his pocket, and mouthed a few words. After the call, he walked over to a large tree and stood behind it.

That's pretty weird. What is he up to?

The sound of a car coming up behind her alerted her to put her camera down and watch through the mirrors. All the glass in Eva's Buick was tinted as dark as it legally could be, limiting what people could see if they looked in.

A blue SUV turned left into the driveway. That was the type of vehicle Mrs. Davenport had said Roxie drove. Eva watched as the SUV parked behind the Mercedes, and a young woman emerged from it and walked to the front door and knocked. Mr. Davenport came out from behind the tree and snuck up on her. He put his arms around her waist, squeezed her, then twirled her around in the air, laughing. Eva was quick with her camera, getting lots of close-ups. When they began to passionately kiss, she zoomed in tight.

After taking a few more pictures of Davenport holding the woman while he unlocked the door, Eva knew she had all the evidence she needed. She watched as they went into the house.

Perfect timing. I can't believe my luck. Just before dark too.

Eva pulled away from the side of the road and continued on down the hill. She enjoyed taking in the view of the hillside and mansions before she drove back to her apartment. She hadn't seen a case that easy in a long time. It would take only a few minutes to upload and email the photographic evidence to Mrs. Davenport. After that, Eva would call Troy to see how he was doing and let him know the good news. She would leave the next morning to go back home.

Chapter 21

Sergeant Mike Stevens had called the police station, requesting Forensics come out there as soon as possible. Collecting fresh evidence would be necessary to identify the two perpetrators. Until then, answering the sergeant's questions about the men was all that would help.

"I wish you'd reconsider and get to the hospital, Troy," Mike pleaded.

Troy paced and couldn't sit still. He wanted to leave in his car and rescue Sadie, but he didn't know where to go. He felt helpless, and a trip to the hospital seemed like a waste of time. "Your concern is appreciated, Mike, but I've been wounded enough to know that I'll be fine. I've stopped the blood loss and cleaned and bandaged the wound. I'm really lucky that it was just a surface wound. The bullet went right through and didn't hit the bone. Last time I was there, they kept me overnight. I can't let that happen now."

Mike shook his head and continued asking Oliver questions. "Oliver, you said that they asked you about the whereabouts of one million four hundred thousand dollars. That was the exact amount, correct?"

The kids wouldn't leave Oliver's side during the questioning.

"Yes, that's right. They asked me where it was hidden."

"Did they give you any reason why they thought it was hidden in this house?"

"No, they didn't. We've only been back here a short time. As you know, this is Sadie and Troy's childhood home. We were living up in Seattle until recently. Lucas Castello, the renter who was living here, was killed in a car accident about a month ago, so we moved back in, wanting to live in a small town in the countryside again."

Sergeant Stevens had his writing pad out and recorded the information. "Was he the only renter that you've had since you moved away? We'll need to know everything that you have on the person who lived here previously. It seems logical that he might have known something about the money. We can run his name and find out if he had a record and who he was associated with."

"Yes, Lucas had lived here for about five years. He paid the rent without fail every month with an automatic deposit into our checking account. We've only met him once, and he seemed like a nice guy. I'm sure I've got a renter's contract on him, stating the type of work he did and other information that we could look up. I don't think I can just sit here, Sergeant Stevens. All I want is to help find my wife. I'll search through her file cabinet and see what I can come up with. She took care of all those details." Oliver stood and walked toward Sadie's office with both kids close behind.

Troy felt agitated. Sitting there answering questions was

not saving his sister, and the sergeant must have noticed him fidgeting.

"I understand how you feel, Troy. But if we got in our vehicles right now, which way would we go? We need a plan. At this point, getting information and details is what will save her. We have to know where to look. Now, Oliver said he never saw their vehicle. Is that right?"

"Yes, they were all blindfolded just minutes after discovering that the men were in the house."

"You said all you know is that it was a dark SUV. Maybe a Denali?"

"That's right. I wasn't able to see the plate number. When they drove off, the garage was in the way of me seeing it."

"Something keeps coming to my mind. Do you remember a few months ago when there was an armored car robbery up north close to Portland? I think it was near a town called Gold Mountain?"

Troy stared at Mike as he recalled reading about it. "Oh my God, Mike. That's right. It was over a million dollars. Yeah, and it was up north, a few months ago. One of the drivers was killed. If I remember right, the other one was in a coma. Do you think the money can be from that robbery?"

"It's a possibility. I'll make a few phone calls to find out for sure. I'll double-check that amount and find out the condition of the other driver and the caliber of the bullets that were used. If we find a bullet here of that same caliber and it's a ballistic match, that will tell us a lot. The one that grazed your shoulder is probably still in that hole in the kitchen wall."

The crunching sound of a vehicle in the driveway caused

them both to look over at the living room window.

"Forensics is here. I'll go let them in," Mike said.

Troy walked into Sadie's office to see how Oliver and the kids were doing. Oliver was looking through the file folder. "Did you find anything that could be helpful?"

"Only basic information on a rental agreement. His full name, age, driver's license number, previous address, and where he went to school. His occupation is stated as freelance writer for a major software company in Portland. There are a couple of names of some of his relatives. I recognize one of them as his uncle, the person who called us upon his death." Oliver handed Troy the paper.

"There's a lot of information here that we could check on. Could I make a couple copies of this on your printer?"

"Of course. I can do some checking, too, and phone calls, whatever would help speed this up."

"Okay, I'll give a copy to Sergeant Stevens and see what would be best to check out first. Willow, honey, could I get the smart watch from you? We may be able to pick up background sounds or something that could help us catch these guys."

Tears were still running down Willow's cheeks as she dabbed at her eyes with the blindfold, which she was wearing around her neck. "I don't have it, Uncle Troy. I put it in Mommy's robe pocket before they took her away. I hope she can get untied and call us."

Troy couldn't believe what he was hearing. He dropped the paper on the floor and pulled out his cell phone. He tapped Willow's smart watch app on his screen. A GPS tracker was one of the options.

Chapter 22

"That was genius, Willow. We can find out where your mom is right now with the GPS that connects my phone to your smart watch. I'm so sorry I didn't think of asking for your watch earlier." Troy poked around on his phone screen until he came up with the smart watch GPS. "She's on Interstate 5, heading north. I'll show the sergeant, and he'll get a BOLO out on it."

Oliver jumped up and looked at Troy's phone screen and then at the kids. All four ran out of the room to find Sergeant Stevens. He was in the backyard talking to the Forensics team. Troy gave him the good news, and Mike immediately called in a BOLO for a dark-colored SUV, possibly a Denali currently on Interstate 5, heading north, approximately twenty miles south of Eugene, Oregon. He let them know the suspects were armed and dangerous and had a female hostage with them.

Mike had a huge smile on his face. "It should only be a matter of time now."

"It's less than two hours away. I'm going to head over to Interstate 5 so I'll be in the vicinity when they find her," Troy told Mike.

Oliver added, "You know the kids and I are going with you, right?"

"Of course, Oliver. I'm sure even if I told you there could be danger, you'd come along, anyway. Mike, I dropped a paper on the office floor. It has information on the renter, Lucas Castello. I know you're staying here with Forensics, but I'll keep in touch by phone with the details. Let's go."

The four of them went outside and climbed into Troy's Jeep. They took off in a hurry. It would be at least an hour and a half before they got to Interstate 5, which would be south of where the GPS showed the smart watch was—where Sadie was.

"Daddy, will we find Mommy soon?" Finn asked as they left the driveway and got onto the road.

"It shouldn't be long now, kids, a couple of hours at the most. We'll bring her back home."

Troy hoped Oliver was right. The family couldn't take a tragedy like that. They needed their mom, Oliver needed his wife, and Troy needed his sister. He glanced at his cell phone, which was set on the GPS app. He saw that they were still heading north. He hoped that before they got to Eugene, the cops would be able to stop any vehicles with the description that Mike had called in. Maybe they were setting up a roadblock. Just then, his phone rang. He glanced at the screen, and it was Eva.

Oh my God, she's going to freak out. "Hey, babe."

"I've got great news. It was the shortest case I've ever been on. The client has the evidence, and I'm out of here after a good night's sleep. I just wanted to let you know I'll be home in the morning."

Troy took a deep breath. He hated to tell her the news. "I've got something to tell you. First of all, I want you to know that I think we have control of the situation."

"What are you talking about? Did you get hurt? Was it the chain saw?"

"It breaks my heart to tell you this, but two men broke into Sadie and Oliver's house before daybreak. They had been holding the family hostage until they found money that was hidden in the house. We're guessing that Lucas, the renter, knew something about it. We think these guys found the money. Oliver and the kids are fine, but they took Sadie with them."

"What? Oh my God, Troy. This can't be happening. Will she be all right? Do you know where she is? Just tell me everything you know."

"The best news that we have right now is that we're tracking them on GPS. Because of that smart watch, which is in Sadie's pocket, we know where they are. At this moment, they're on Interstate 5, heading north toward Eugene. We've got a BOLO out on a dark SUV, maybe a Denali. Since we have their exact location, they could be stopped at any moment. The other details, I can tell you about later, but Oliver, the kids, and I are on our way to Interstate 5, and we'll head north."

"Okay, I'll leave Portland, jump on the freeway, and head south. I'll keep in touch and pray for the best." Eva ended the call.

Troy continued to drive, keeping within the speed limit. The last thing they needed was to get pulled over. He decided to hand the phone to Oliver so he could watch the GPS and pick up any calls that might come through while Troy concentrated on driving. He glanced at the time on his dash. They should hit the interstate within one hour, and it couldn't come soon enough. If they hurt Sadie, he didn't know what he would do. He was sure Oliver felt the same way.

Every once in a while, Troy could hear the kids in the back seat, crying softly and talking to each other in quiet voices. He was proud of his niece and nephew. In just a few hours, they had been through more than most kids would go through in a lifetime. Oliver kept turning to the back seat to see how they were doing and console them.

Oliver was looking at Troy's phone when he gasped. "Oh my God, Troy, they've pulled off of Interstate 5. They're on Highway 126."

"Quick, call Mike. Tell him what they did."

Troy could see Oliver scrolling through the phone then heard him say, "Mike, this is Oliver. We still have them on GPS tracking, and they just turned off onto Highway 126, heading east. Yes, good, thanks."

"He said he'll let the officials know to extend the BOLO. That will narrow it down. It's better this way. Smaller road, less traffic. They'll get them."

"Great, I hope Sadie can hold up okay. I know she will, because she knows how much all of us love her. It won't be long now, Oliver. Soon, Mike will call to tell us that they've been stopped. Go ahead and call Eva. Tell her where they've turned."

Troy hit Interstate 5, got into the northbound lane, and sped up. He headed toward Eugene then east on Highway 126. Between the highway patrol with the BOLO, Eva headed south, and Troy headed north, the men would be surrounded soon.

Oliver stared at the phone's screen, "Oh my God, Troy. The app on your phone shows that the watch's battery power is at five percent. It's in the red."

Chapter 23

Eva's phone rang. She glanced at the screen, and it was Troy. She answered and put him on Speaker. "Any good news yet?"

"Eva, it's me, Oliver. I'm tracking the GPS on the smart watch with Troy's phone so he can concentrate on driving. They turned off on Highway 126 heading east. This was five minutes ago. Mike has already extended the BOLO to that area. And the bad news is, the battery on the watch is down to five percent."

"Damn, I'm glad you were able to see that they turned off the interstate, but where they end up when the battery goes dead is going to be anybody's guess. I know that road heads off into national forest land. There will be lots of narrow roads and campgrounds coming up."

"Yeah, we're worried about that too. There are a lot of roads they can branch off on from 126. That road heads east for a while and then turns north to a ski area. The road that continues east, 242, is closed in winter, so they won't be going that way."

Eva tried to picture that area. "You know, Oliver, the best thing for me to do is get off the interstate at the city of

Albany, which is coming up in about half an hour. I'll take Highway 20. It goes southeast and connects to 126 just before the ski resort. If we're lucky, they'll be driving somewhere in between you guys and myself. Tell Troy. Let me know if anything changes."

"Got it."

I hope this is the right decision.

Eva drove at the top of the speed limit and then a little over as she passed as many cars and semitrucks as she came upon. She couldn't imagine why the men took Sadie. If they had already found the money, why they felt the need to take her was a mystery. Eva was told that the family never saw the men's faces, so she didn't think the men would worry about being identified. Eva was thinking about Sadie's fear of open spaces. If she had the chance to get away, her love of family should overcome the panic attacks and help her succeed. Maybe. Eva wasn't a psychologist, but she was a woman with a strong love of family. Her instinct was that Sadie was as well.

She was coming up on Albany and watched for the Highway 20 East exit. It was getting late in the day. They needed to find the SUV before dark. With all the mountains around her, the light would leave the valley faster than it did at the coast.

There it was. She saw the exit, put on her blinker, and got off the interstate. It was time to speed up and watch for a dark-colored SUV heading her way. At that point, Troy would be behind them and coming toward her. She wasn't sure where the highway patrol was, probably somewhere in between them. Eva had complete confidence that anytime, her sister-in-law would be rescued. She sped up while she drove along a straightaway. It had been a while since she had been on that road, but she remembered that a lot of curves were coming up. She glanced at her dash.

Damn, I'm almost on empty.

If her memory was correct, there would be a gas station a few miles down the road. She knew the gas gauge gave her ample warning. She glanced down to see if there were any more messages on her phone. There weren't, and she continued driving. Soon, she saw the station on the right-hand side of the road. Eva put on her blinkers and pulled in.

"Hello. Fill it up and please hurry," she told the attendant. After pulling four twenties out of her purse, she gave them to him and said to keep the change. He smiled and began to clean the windshield. Eva reminded him that she needed to leave. As he nodded, a dark-colored SUV passed by—a Denali.

Oh my God, that could be it.

She yelled at the attendant, "Sorry, please move!" He backed away from her Buick. Eva spun the wheel hard, stepped on the gas, and sped off in the opposite direction from which she'd come.

She caught up with the car and followed closely but not so close as to arouse suspicion. She tried to see through the car's back window. There were silhouettes of two people in the front seat. The person on the passenger side was slumped against the door. Eva felt for the phone on her lap and pressed Troy's contact.

Oliver answered, "Yes, Eva."

I'm following a dark Denali SUV on Highway 20. I was at a gas station when I saw it go by. Now I'm turned around and have them in my sight, heading west. I'm right behind it but unable to see the full license number yet. All I can see is that it's an Oregon plate and it begins with, well, sorry, I can't make out any numbers or letters. Go ahead and call it in. Denali, SUV, west, on Highway 20."

"Got it. I'll do that right away. Thank God you saw it. The watch battery has died. If that is them, we would've had no idea that they turned off there. Hopefully, the highway patrol can intercept."

"I'll keep in touch with you whenever I can. I know the cell service starts getting sporadic in this area."

"Okay, be safe. I'll call that in now."

She continued to follow, knowing that the road branched off into remote areas. She had to stay close but without being noticed. They were headed for a curvy section of road that would quickly rise in elevation.

Chapter 24

Adam's mind was made up. She would drown in the cold, dark lake. He would weight her body down and stab her in the lungs first to let the air out. He remembered watching a movie once where the killers were ready to throw a body into a lake. One of them told the other to be sure to pierce the lungs so the corpse wouldn't float to the surface.

He was tired. He couldn't believe all that had happened over the last twenty-four hours. He wanted it to be over with but knew he had to be careful. There could be no more mistakes. Gabe was dead, so it was all up to him now. He watched for Trail Top Road. The sooner he got off Highway 20, the better he would feel. Then it would be another forty-five minutes of back road driving before he arrived at Gabe's cabin. That time of year, he'd probably have the whole lake to himself. That was what he needed to get rid of evidence and to get rid of bodies.

Who would have thought it would come to this? It was supposed to be a simple plan.

He counted the dead since it all started—the armored car driver, Lucas, Gabe, and soon, this woman. She would be the only one to die at his hand.

There it was, Trail Top Road. He glanced in his rearview mirror, saw headlights, and put on his signal. After he completed his turn, he noticed the car was still behind him.

Am I being followed?

He kept an eye on it then had to laugh at himself. He was getting paranoid. It was a public road, and anyone could drive on it. Darkness had fallen, and he couldn't tell what kind of car it was or who was driving. All he could see were the headlights.

Then the woman started up again. "When are you going to let me go? I can't harm you. I'm no good to you. Just leave me on the side of the road."

"I don't want to hear anything else out of you. I told you before to shut up. I'll let you go when I'm ready, not when you tell me to."

At some point before he got to the cabin, he would have to pull off the road and put a gag on her. It was a precaution he would have to take in case another house on the lake was occupied. Sound amplified as it traveled across water. He couldn't take the chance that someone might be staying out there and hear her screams.

"I just need a drink of water. Please, I'm so thirsty."

He realized that would be a perfect excuse to pull over and gag her. She would think he was going to give her a drink and wouldn't scream until it was too late.

He reached into his pocket to get out the handkerchief that he'd dried his face with earlier. He needed something else though, too, something to put in her mouth first to completely muffle any sounds after he gagged her. Looking across the front seat at Gabe, he noticed a handkerchief clutched in his hand.

Perfect.

"Okay, I've got a bottle of water up here. As soon as I find a place to pull over, I'll stop and give you a drink."

He watched the side of the road for a wide spot on the shoulder. When he found one a couple of miles up, he put on his signal and pulled over. Adam didn't get out until the car behind him passed by slowly.

What the hell are they looking at? People need to mind their own business.

After grabbing the water bottle and both handkerchiefs, he got out, opened the back door, and reached in. When he touched her, she jumped.

"Hold on there. Be still. I'm just trying to help you sit up, then I'll give you a drink. I'm going to grab onto your arm and pull you over so you're sitting on the seat. When you feel the bottle touch your lips, then take a drink."

He decided to let her have a couple of sips before he gagged her. She swallowed rapidly. He took the bottle away from her then quickly stuffed one of the handkerchiefs into her mouth. She bit down hard on his hand and screamed.

Adam pulled away. "You bitch!" He formed a fist and struck her squarely in the jaw.

She jerked away from him at the force of his punch. He pulled her to him by her hair and held her head between his forearm and chest as he swung the other handkerchief around her mouth. He gave it an extra-hard tug as he tied it in a knot. There would be no way she could get it off. He checked the zip ties that constrained her wrists and the ropes that were around her ankles. Everything was still tight. Then he looked at his hand, which was bleeding.

Damn her, human bites are the worst. He wiped the blood onto his pants.

A growl came from deep inside her throat as she jerked and tried to get away. Adam watched her for a minute, admiring her gumption. It was time to finish the drive, get to the cabin, and dump the bodies in the lake. He still had to clean the blood out of his car and put in a few more hours on the road before the long day was over. Then he would be at home, safe and rich.

After he got in the driver's seat, he stepped hard on the gas pedal, anxious to get to the cabin. About a mile down the road, he noticed a car pulled off onto a side road. The front of it was facing the road, which told him that they had backed in and were waiting for him to drive by. Someone knew what he was up to.

Two can play at this game.

He sped up, taking the curves as fast as possible. He had to lose them and get to the cabin quickly. Finally, he saw the driveway entrance. After pulling in, he turned the wheel all the way to the left and stepped hard on the gas, causing the SUV to spin in a circle and face the entrance. He turned off the headlights and watched.

After sitting there for fifteen minutes, he realized he was being paranoid. No cars went past the driveway. He drove his SUV close to the cabin, got out, and walked around the outside of it to find a way to break in. The bedroom window looked like it would be easy to climb into. He picked up a large rock and smashed it. Then he knocked out the shards of glass that stuck to the casing. After he climbed in, he walked to the kitchen to mentally make a list of what he needed. To start, he needed lots of rags to soak up the blood, trash bags, and a bucket of hot water. He would need disinfectant with bleach, which he'd probably find under the sink. It would be best to get rid of the bodies first then clean everything up. If he got blood on his clothes, he'd have to get rid of those, too, and wear something from Gabe's closet. Not that it would fit. He thought about it, and if Gabe had coveralls somewhere, he could just put those on over his own clothes.

He walked to the bedroom closet and opened the door. Sure enough, there were a couple of pairs of coveralls folded and placed on a shelf. Adam grabbed a pair, crawled into them, and pulled the zipper up tight against his neck. He couldn't carry Gabe all the way down to the lake. The woman would be easy. A wheelbarrow would work great, or he could use a tarp to roll Gabe out and slide him on the ground to the dock. Then he would push him off the dock and into the boat, row out to the middle of the lake, and dump him. He'd need bricks or rocks to weight them down and ropes to tie the weights to their bodies.

Adam walked to the attached garage. There, he found everything he needed, even the wheelbarrow. He planned to get Gabe's body out of the way first since he was spilling way too much blood in the SUV. Adam unfolded a tarp and laid it out over the wheelbarrow. He picked up a fillet knife from the workbench. It had a five-inch blade and looked like it had been recently sharpened. A stack of bricks was lined up against the back door. Adam remembered that Gabe had talked about using them to build an outdoor kitchen on the back patio. Adam put a few bricks in the wheelbarrow along with a coil of rope and the knife. He found another tarp and tossed it in the wheelbarrow with the other items. He would use the second tarp to wrap the woman. He didn't want to see her face when he dumped her into the murky water.

Deciding he had everything he needed, he pushed the wheelbarrow out of the garage door and over to the SUV. First, he opened the back door to check on the woman. She wasn't moving, and it looked like she had fallen asleep. He went over to the front passenger side and opened that door slowly. Gabe's body leaned on the door. Adam put his hand out against Gabe's shoulder and held it still while he opened the door wider. With his other hand, he grabbed the front of the wheelbarrow and pulled it toward him to line it up with Gabe's body. He let go of the shoulder and watched as the front half of Gabe's body slid into the wheelbarrow. He reached out and pulled Gabe toward him by his belt to get him completely out of the car. Gabe's body fell into the wheelbarrow with a *thud*.

Another pool of blood dripped from the car seat onto the floor. Adam felt his stomach churning. He looked away quickly, pulled the wheelbarrow back from the car, and closed the door. The moon was full. He could see the path to the dock as he pushed the wheelbarrow toward the lake.

Gabe's rowboat was tied up securely at both ends and close to the dock. Adam was relieved to see the oars were in it. He wrapped Gabe's body in the tarp, tied a rope around his chest and hips, and pulled tight. The other end of the ropes secured the bricks.

The task that Adam dreaded most was next. He gripped the knife and thrust it hard through the tarp and into Gabe's chest. He stabbed Gabe four times, wanting to make sure his lungs were pierced. If he had done everything right, Gabe's body would be at the bottom of the lake for a very long time. Adam tipped up the end of the wheelbarrow and dumped the body into the rowboat. After he untied the ropes from the pylons and tossed them in the boat, he stepped in and pushed off. He searched the perimeter of the lake to see if any lights were on in the homes. There was no sign any of them were occupied. Thankful that half of the ordeal was over, he gripped the oars and rowed. He still had a lot to do, all of it under the cover of darkness. It was going to be a long night.

Chapter 25

After the Denali went past, Eva waited a minute before continuing to follow. A full moon lit up the road enough that she could see her way without turning on her headlights. She sped up, needing to get close enough to keep the SUV in sight. There it was. She saw the back fender as it turned in to a driveway. There was a wide spot on the side of the road. She quickly pulled over and parked. It was time to call Troy and let him know what she was going to do. She pressed the home button on her phone—no service.

Once she knew Troy wouldn't be aware of what she was going to do, Eva felt completely alone. It was time to think of a plan. That SUV could belong to anyone. If she was seen sneaking around, the cops could be called, or worse yet, she could be shot at. She would have a lot of explaining to do. But if that was the vehicle that held Sadie, nothing was more important than rescuing her. Eva remembered that her glove compartment held a flashlight with a night vision option. Hoping the batteries would still have power, she took it out and turned it on.

This will work.

The light that shone from it had a soft red glow. That made it easy for her to see where she was going but wasn't as intrusive as a glaring white light from a regular flashlight. It had the basic light option, too, in case it was needed. The compartment also held a leather case with her hunting knife. She took that out and clipped it on her waistband. Eva reached under her seat, pulled out her loaded Glock, and tucked it securely behind her belt.

Time to go. Reaching up to the overhead console, she turned off the interior light switch so the car would stay dark when she opened the door. After she took the keys out of the ignition and put them in her pocket, she quietly got out. As she pointed the flashlight straight down at the ground, she walked carefully through the woods, toward the driveway. Standing behind a tree for cover, she peered around it and saw the SUV parked next to a cabin. She flipped off the flashlight. There was no need for it since she could see her way. Staying close to the edge of the driveway, she continued on. When she approached the car, she leaned against the fender and peered in the back window.

Oh my God, that's Sadie.

Eva quickly looked around to see if anyone else was in sight. No one. She quietly opened the car door. It was hard to believe what she was looking at. Sadie was not only blindfolded and gagged but tied with a rope around her ankles, and her wrists were bound behind her.

The first thing Eva did was pull her blindfold off. Sadie's eyes were wide with fear.

"Sadie, don't worry. It's me, Eva. We have to talk quietly.

I'll cut your bindings off, and you can come with me."

Eva pulled the gag off and reached in to pull out the handkerchief lodged inside Sadie's mouth. Sadie whimpered. "Eva, is that really you? Are my kids okay? Where's Oliver?"

"Yes, everyone's fine. They're in the car with Troy right now. They're driving this way to find you. We have to be quiet. I'm going to free your arms and legs. It's a short walk to my car, and then we can get out of here."

She rolled Sadie over onto her stomach and pulled the hunting knife from its case. Eva knew that the poor woman's arms were going to hurt when they were freed. The zip ties were so tight that it was hard to get a knife blade in between Sadie's swollen wrists without cutting her skin.

"The bastards that did this to you are going to burn in hell. Do you know where they are right now?"

"I think one of them is dead. There were gunshots back at the house. While they were driving, I heard them talking about trying to stay alive and all the blood one of them was losing. The other one, from the sounds that I heard, is probably getting rid of the body."

"I'm sorry if I accidentally cut your skin. I have to get around to the other side of the car to cut the ropes on your legs. Then we can go."

Eva hurried, opened the door, and stuck the blade under the ropes binding Sadie's ankles. She had to cut them in a sawing motion since the blade was dull.

"Okay, you're free. I know you're going to be sore. Can you move your arms and legs?"

Sadie didn't answer.

Eva watched as she slowly stretched her ankles and moved them in a circular motion. "I'm going to reach in and rub your legs. We need to get the blood circulating again. Then I'll help you sit up. As soon as you feel as though you can put weight on your feet, we'll get out of here."

Eva could tell that Sadie was having a hard time putting any pressure on her hands. She crawled in the back seat and put her arms under Sadie's body to help her turn over and sit up.

"I feel dizzy. I don't know if I can do this."

"I'm sorry, but you have to. Our lives are at stake. We have to get to my car and get out of here."

Eva put her arms tightly around Sadie's waist and pulled her up from the floor to a sitting position on the back seat. Eva eyed the area outside of the SUV, looking for any signs of movement.

"Okay, we'll sit here for a minute." Eva was nervous about Sadie's ability to get out of the car, both physically and mentally. She decided to focus on the physical part, and hopefully, Sadie would overcome her fear. Eva took Sadie's left arm and gently put her hands around it and squeezed then rubbed. She reached across Sadie's chest and did the same with her right arm.

"How are your legs feeling? Are they still numb?"

"No, the numbness is going away. I think the circulation is coming back in my arms too."

Eva was surprised. She knew Sadie had been tied up since that morning. Next, she had to talk her out of the car and take a walk through the woods.

"I'll help you stand now. Let's scoot across the seat, and I'll get out first and reach in to help you out of the car. I'll hang on to you until you feel like you have your balance. I have a very dim flashlight so we can see our way to my car. It won't be long now until you'll be back with Oliver and the kids, who love you. They're worried about you, and we can show them that you're okay."

Eva slid across the seat to the open door. She hung onto Sadie and helped her to scoot along. After backing out to stand on the ground, Eva reached in to get Sadie.

"I don't think I can do this. I can't go outside." Sadie's breathing came fast and shallow. "I'm getting dizzy again. I think I'm going to faint."

Eva didn't know whether to yell at her or sympathize with her. It was a real thing, agoraphobia—real to someone mentally, at least. But they were in a physically dangerous situation. Eva had to get Sadie out of there and fast.

"Please, Sadie. We have to go now. You can close your eyes if you want. My car isn't far. I'll lead you."

Sadie nodded, giving the impression she understood and would try. Eva saw Sadie close her eyes as tears rolled down her cheeks. She kept an arm around Sadie's waist as she pulled her tightly against her side. Sadie looked as though she was trying to straighten her legs to stand. Eva was elated—it was going to work, and they would get away safely. Then she heard a sound behind her. The snap of a branch brought her emotions crashing down. She looked at Sadie, whose eyes focused on something over her shoulder and opened wide in obvious fear. It happened so fast. Eva didn't feel it, but she heard it, and something hard cracked against her skull. Then she felt the weightlessness of falling.

Chapter 26

Frustration was taking over, and Troy didn't know what to do. When the smart watch battery died, it showed that the men who had Sadie were heading north on Highway 126. It had been dark for two hours. The last time they'd talked to Eva, she was on Highway 20. She'd told him she was at a gas station when she saw a dark Denali pass by. She turned around and followed it, heading west. The BOLO that encompassed a large area of Highway 126, Highway 20, and part of Interstate 5 hadn't led to any leads.

"Oliver, will you try to call Eva again?"

"Sure, she's been out of cell service for a while. Hopefully, we can reach her now." Oliver touched the contact for Eva and listened. "No luck. It goes right to voicemail. I'll try Mike again."

He called Mike and got what he'd expected to hear. Oliver relayed the message to Troy.

"No luck on the BOLO or any sightings. The cops pulled over three Denalis that were dark in color, but nothing was suspicious. Mike mentioned that the BOLO would tighten up at the gas station that Eva called from and then west to

Interstate 5. He would put patrols north and south on that interstate."

"Daddy, I miss Mommy. When will we find her? Do we have anything to eat?" Finn cried out from the back seat.

"I'm sorry, Finn. We're still looking for Mommy, but we'll stop and get some food. Willow, honey, are you okay?"

"I'm just worried, Dad. I'm worried that we won't find Mom."

Troy was concerned about the kids' well-being, and he was sure Oliver was too. "You know what I'm thinking, you two? I'm thinking that we should get a hot dinner and a couple of motel rooms. You guys have been through a lot, and you need some rest. I have my laptop computer with me, and I can check some things out on it."

Oliver reluctantly agreed. Driving around aimlessly wasn't beneficial. They could take care of the kids and research the armored car robbery. Troy's phone would be available for either Mike or Eva to call them with any information. Troy saw a sign for a motel and restaurants at the next exit. He pulled off the highway and drove up to the entrance of a Holiday Inn and parked.

"I'll go in and get a couple rooms," Troy said before he walked toward the motel office. After talking to the clerk, he got the keys for two adjoining rooms on the first floor. He went to the car and helped Oliver walk the kids to their room.

"I see a grocery store close by and a pizza place next to it. I'll get us some food and be back as soon as I can," Troy said.

Troy went to the pizza restaurant first and ordered a large

combination. While it baked, he went to the store and picked up fresh fruit, milk, and bottles of water. He felt bad that the day had gone by without finding Sadie. It broke his heart to think of what could be happening to her. Oliver and the kids had gone through hell too.

Troy's phone sounded, and his heart leapt, thinking it was Eva. It wasn't. Mike was calling to say he was checking into a motel in the Albany area, on Interstate 5.

"I wish something would have come up on the BOLO, Troy. How is everyone holding up?"

"We just now checked into a motel about an hour east of where you're at, on Highway 20. The kids needed food and rest. It's really been an emotional day for them, and they're worried about Sadie, of course."

"Have you heard from Eva lately? Is she calling it quits for the night?" Mike asked.

"I've been waiting, but I haven't heard from her in over an hour. I'm guessing she's been out of cell service area, because her phone goes right to voicemail. But if she's still on Highway 20, she should have been back in a cell service area by now. I hope nothing's happened, but I'll call you the minute I do hear from her. I'm going to do a computer search for the details of that armed robbery in Gold Mountain a few months ago. I'll let you know if I find anything at all." Troy ended his call with Mike and took the food into Oliver's room.

The pizza didn't last long since no one had eaten since the day before. It was hard to believe that yesterday was Christmas. So much had happened. Going from a joyous day to complete terror had to be hard on everyone.

"Willow, would you pour a glass of milk for your brother and yourself, please? I'd like it if you each ate a banana or an apple before you go to bed too," Oliver said.

"Sure, Dad, I will. Are the police still looking for Mom?"

"They sure are, and they'll find her too. Don't you worry about that. We'll get some rest, and then we'll help the police again tomorrow," Oliver told his daughter.

Troy walked over to Finn and Willow and gave them a big hug. "Kids, with so many people looking for your mom, I'm sure she'll be found soon. We don't want you guys to worry. Your mom would want you to get a lot of rest so you can help us find her tomorrow. Good night, now."

Troy promised to wake Oliver if he found out anything. Then he said good night and went to his room.

His laptop was already fully charged. Troy had brought it in from the Jeep after he checked in at the office. He set his phone next to it and began his research.

Chapter 27

"Damn it, who is this woman, and why is she here?" Adam shouted.

Sadie didn't answer. Her eyes were wild as she sat on the seat and slid away from him. He kept screaming questions at her.

"Do you know her? How did she find this place? I'm talking to you. I better get an answer, or I'll find a way to make you talk."

Adam grabbed the woman by her arm and dragged her away from the car. A pool of blood began to form on the ground from the large gash on the side of her head.

This one's not going anywhere. I'll take care of the other one first.

He looked at Sadie. "I can whack you with this branch, too, if you don't start talking."

"I don't know her or how she got here. She just appeared," she sobbed.

Adam didn't believe her, but it made no difference. The woman was there. A gun was on the ground next to the car door. He picked it up, looked it over, then dropped it into his jacket pocket.

What else does this bitch have?

He rolled her over onto her stomach and checked her jacket pockets for identification. There was no wallet or phone. He found a set of car keys and a flashlight. Using it, he checked the ground around the car to see if anything else had been dropped. Something shiny caught his eye. A hunting knife—that was what she'd cut Sadie loose with. He picked it up and turned to look at the woman. He wasn't sure if she was dead or out cold, but it was time to find out. When he kicked her in the ribs, a deep moan came from her throat. Now he had two women to deal with.

Where did she leave her car? She had to be the one that was following me. It couldn't be more than a mile away.

First things first, the women had to be contained while he looked for the car. If it was discovered along the road, someone might show up there snooping around. Adam remembered that a cellar was on the property somewhere. Gabe had dug one a few years ago, using the cool underground room as a wine cellar and for storing canned goods. A few years ago, Adam had helped Gabe stack cinder blocks against the walls while he was there on a fishing weekend. He looked around the property and remembered the cellar was on the east side of the garage. That was where he would keep the women until he decided whether to leave them or kill them.

He had to contain one of them while he got the other one down. The rope tied around Sadie's ankles had been cut, but there were two lengths that looked long enough to use to temporarily tie up the woman on the ground until he could get back to her. He grabbed the rope from the floor of the back seat. The woman was still lying on her stomach. Adam pulled her arms together and wrapped the rope around her wrists. He used the other piece to secure her ankles. It was time to get Sadie. She was small enough to just drag if needed. He reached into the back seat of the car and grabbed her arm. She struggled and screamed.

"Look, lady, this is going to happen whether you like it or not." He picked up the bandanna from the seat. "You're making it harder on yourself. Relax, I'm just putting you somewhere else. Shut up, and you'll stay alive."

He threw the bandanna around her head and made sure the knot was tight. It muffled her screams while he dragged her out of the car toward the cellar. She dug her heels into the dirt and tried to stop him.

When he got to the garage, he dragged her inside with him to find something to tie her wrists. A long length of rope was tied to a buoy. Adam took the hunting knife out of his pocket and cut the rope off and then in half.

"Roll over on your stomach," he ordered as he let go of Sadie's arm.

She got on her hands and knees and crawled away from him toward the door. Adam walked along next to her, shaking his head in disbelief. His foot came down hard on her back, causing her body to flatten against the cement floor. He pulled her arms together, flipped the rope around her wrists, and tied it in a knot.

"Stop kicking your legs. The sooner you cooperate, the less painful things will get." He pushed down her legs and tied the rope around her ankles.

Leaving her, he went out the door to find the cellar entrance. When he scanned the flashlight along the ground, he saw the wooden door that was angled against the wall of the garage. A metal shaft placed through the lock hasp was all that kept it closed. Using the handle of the hunting knife, he knocked the rusty metal shaft out of the hasp. The wooden door creaked on its hinges as he opened it. Adam shined the flashlight in front of him as he walked down the steps into the cellar. He remembered that a light hung from the ceiling and pulled the chain.

As he looked around, he spotted the shelf filled with canned goods, the wine rack with a few dusty bottles, and not much else. It would work as a place to keep them while he found the woman's car and cleaned the blood from his.

He went back into the garage to get Sadie. She was still sobbing as he picked her up and threw her over his shoulder. She didn't weigh much, but it was difficult to get her down the narrow opening. When he got to the last step, he pushed her to the dirt floor. Adam stood there for a moment and caught his breath. As he turned to go up the stairs to get the other woman, he hollered to Sadie, "Take it easy. You'll soon have company."

Chapter 28

As Eva returned to consciousness, the pain enveloped her. It felt like her brain was on fire, and her eyelids were heavy as she tried to open them. When she did, the trees around her seemed tilted at a crazy angle. Eva wasn't sure if she could move her body to stand.

What happened? Where am I?

Blood spewed from her mouth as she coughed and tried to clear her lungs. When her eyes fully opened, the shine from the bumper of a car came into focus. Eva thought she'd been in a car accident. Her mind was spinning, trying to remember if anyone else was riding with her.

Sadie, that's who it was. Sadie was in the car.

Then it all came back to her. Sadie was in trouble, and Eva had been trying to coax her out of the car when something hit her on the head. Eva knew she had to get to a standing position and make sure Sadie was okay. She bent her lower legs and tried to roll onto her side to stand. Once on her hands and knees, she was in a crawling position. It was an accomplishment. Next, she put pressure on her feet and looked for something to hang onto while she tried to stand upright. The car's bumper was right beside her. She pushed down on it with her hand and got to her feet. Eva stayed close to the side of the car as she made her way to the back door and opened it.

It was empty. She glanced toward the front seats—no Sadie. Eva knew she wouldn't have run off on her own. Someone had her, and it was up to Eva to find out who. When she reached to her waistband to grab her gun, she was terrified to discover it gone.

Where are my knife and flashlight?

She put her hand in her jacket pocket but touched no car keys. Whoever had hit her over the head must have grabbed everything, including Sadie. It was time to take cover and look around. Eva felt a wave of dizziness as she pushed away from the car's fender and walked to the nearest tree. Standing behind it, she took in her surroundings. The car that had once held Sadie was in front of her. It was the Denali that she had been following. A small, dimly lit cabin stood thirty yards away. A light was shining from the top of a pole next to the garage. The full moon reflected on a large lake, which was at least one hundred yards away.

The best thing to do would be to stay in the shadows, get close to the cabin, and look in the windows to search for Sadie, but Eva realized she had no weapon. It might be a better idea to get back to her car and drive until she got to cell phone service. Then, she could get the cops, sheriff, Troy, and everyone to go out there. But the fact was that she didn't have the keys. She wished she knew how to hot-wire a car. Eva swore to herself that if she and Sadie got out of that situation, she would learn to hot-wire, and she would sign up for a self-defense class.

Trees lined the way to the cabin. Eva stood close to them as she walked toward it, hoping she wouldn't pass out from the shooting pain that ripped through her head. Within a couple of minutes, she was up against the side of the garage, away from the yard light. Walking around the back of it, she stayed close to the wall and peered in each window as she came to it. It didn't look like anything was going on in the garage. A few steps across the walkway and she was up against the house, making her way to the first window. She peered around and looked inside. It was the main room of the cabin. A man stood by the front door, looking down at a set of keys that he held. He twirled them in his fingers. They were her keys—she could tell by the blue whale charm on the chain. Next, he clicked on a flashlight—her flashlight. She was relieved when she saw him walk out the front door.

Eva stayed close to the side of the house as she walked quietly to the end of it and looked around the corner. The man was lit by the yard light as he walked toward the Denali. He was tall, and his jacket and pants were dark colored. His tennis shoes squeaked when he walked, as if they had recently been in the water.

The thought crossed her mind that he could have drowned Sadie in the lake. Eva quickly made that idea go away. It was time to get in the cabin and look for her. She could be tied up inside one of the rooms. Eva remembered seeing two people in the front seat when she was following them, and someone else could be inside.

The next room was the kitchen. Nothing unusual was going on in there. She continued to the last two windows of the small cabin. Both were bedrooms, and they were empty. The back door was next. She tried the doorknob. It wasn't locked. As she quietly opened the door and stepped inside, she knew she had to search the place quickly before he got back. Both bedrooms and their closets were empty. She made her way through the rest of the house, completely aware that the other man could be in there somewhere. In the main room, she saw a fireplace tool set on the hearth. Something in that could be used as a weapon. She picked up the heavy iron poker and kept it over her shoulder as she continued to search. Eva looked for a basement door, another place to keep someone captive. No luck. She decided to go outside, take cover, and watch for the man to return.

Eva left from the back door, hurried to the nearest tree, and stood behind it. Then she heard him.

"Where are you? Where the hell are you, bitch? You might as well come out now. You know I'll find you, anyway."

She stood still and watched. He entered through the front door and slammed it behind him. Obscenities came through loud and clear as he searched the house for her. Then everything got quiet. Eva walked farther into the woods. She wanted to be away from the house but still have a vantage point to watch from. Then she saw him. He came out of the back door with the flashlight on its most powerful setting, shining it into the woods. She moved to a larger tree and turned sideways, trying to make herself small. She prayed he wouldn't see her.

"Hey, lady, I know you're out there. Come out now, and I won't be so hard on you. I'll even let your little friend go."

Eva hoped that meant Sadie was still alive and all right. It could just be a ploy to get her out of the woods. She stood still. Footsteps crunched on the dead leaves. He was coming her way. She closed her eyes tight, trying to make the horror disappear. He was close to the tree where she hid. All she could do was raise the poker up high and hope for the chance to take him by surprise.

Eva waited. The footsteps stopped. She couldn't tell which side of the tree he was going to come around. She felt as if he knew she was there. Eva was right, and the cold steel of a gun pressed up hard against her neck.

"Oh, I see you found a weapon. Well, you might as well drop it. The gun at your neck is much more lethal. Now move it. Throw it down and start walking toward the cabin. I'm not known for having a lot of patience."

She was defeated. She still held the poker, and the thought came to mind that she could spin around quickly and try to slap the gun out of his hand before he could pull the trigger. A harder press from the gun barrel against her neck changed her mind. She dropped the poker.

"Now walk, head toward the garage, and don't stop until I tell you to."

Her mind raced. She hadn't searched the garage, so maybe Sadie was in there. Eva walked slowly in front of him. He prodded her with the barrel of the gun to coax her on. When they got to the door, he told her to keep walking.

After a few paces, he said, "Now sit down on the ground over by the wall."

Eva did as told, bracing for something painful. Was he going to shoot her there or knock her out again? To her surprise, he walked over to an angled door. He kept the gun on her while he opened it and pushed up the lid.

"Before you see your friend, you can make it easier on yourself by answering a couple of questions. How do you know her, and how did you find me?"

Eva sat and glared at him. "Go to hell, you bastard. What did you do to her? She better be all right, or I swear to God, you'll pay with your life."

"Well, I guess that means you're not going to answer. As of right now, she's traumatized but alive. I'm still trying to decide what I want to do with you both. Let's see how these next few minutes go. Now stand up. Get over here and climb down the steps."

Eva was anxious to see Sadie but afraid that once she got down there, they would have no way to escape. She looked around for anything lying on the ground that she could throw at him, anything to distract him. A rock next to her hand could do some damage if she threw it at him. Eva lowered her head in a look of defeat. Grasping the rock with her left hand, she held it firmly and pushed herself up from the ground. He waved her gun toward the cellar, signaling for her to walk that way. She took that opportunity to take aim and throw the rock as hard as she could at his face. It caught him on the side of his head, and he fell backward and hit the ground hard. Eva ran for the gun, but it was too late. When she got to him, he had it pointed at her.

"I'll give you one thing, woman, you've got gumption.

Now move it and be glad I don't shoot you where you stand."

Eva was surprised he didn't kill her right then. She did as he demanded, knowing that she would think of another way of escape later. She just wanted to see Sadie and make sure she was okay. Eva walked to the entrance. A dim light shone from the cellar below. She could see rope-bound feet next to the corner of a shelf. It had to be Sadie.

Eva walked down the steps. When she got to the last one, she heard the loud crash of the door being slammed above her. Then came the sound of metal against metal as they were locked in. She hurried to Sadie, kneeled beside her, and removed the bandanna from her mouth. "Sadie, it's Eva. Are you all right?"

Sadie opened her eyes and turned toward her. "Thank God you're here."

Chapter 29

That will keep them contained for a while.

Adam grew tired of redoing his plan. That woman had changed everything. All he would have had to do was get rid of Sadie's body, clean the blood out of the car, and dump evidence in the lake. He would have been able to get away without leaving a clue that he had ever been there. It was time to go get the car, and it couldn't be too far away. It bothered him that he hadn't found out how she'd known to follow him. The car's registration might tell him something. He clicked on the flashlight, made sure he still had her keys in his pocket, and headed into the woods. He continued toward the road, walked parallel to it, and stayed among the trees in case someone drove by and saw him. The moonlight reflected off a car parked on the side of the road. That had to be hers.

Adam pulled the keys out of his pocket and pressed the fob. The headlights blinked.

Just as I thought. She wasn't far away.

He got in the front seat and turned on the ignition. He drove the short distance to the cabin and parked behind the garage and as close to the trees as possible. The longer it took someone to find the car, the better. At least it couldn't be seen from the road. Adam opened the glove compartment, took out the registration, and read.

The car was registered to a Troy and Eva Winters. The names didn't ring a bell. There was no connection to Sadie and Oliver that he could think of. Then he glanced at the residence address—New Haven, Oregon. That was a small coastal town close to Elk River, where Lucas lived and where the money was. Maybe they were friends or relatives. It really didn't matter. That paper was just one more thing to throw in the lake. The license plates would be another. He would grab a screwdriver and remove them to add to his bag of disposable evidence. Adam knew that removing the plates would only stall whoever found the car. They could get the identification number off it and do a little research, and the owner's name would pop up. But the more time it took, the better his chance of being out of the country when everything was found, including the bodies.

The cupboard under the kitchen sink held all that he needed for the cleanup. He found rags, disinfectant, and a bucket for hot water. A stiff scrubbing brush and a box of trash bags from the drawer completed his list of items. Some of the blood had probably dried on the carpet. He took everything out to the Denali and began to work. First, he checked his bags of money in the back. That gave him the incentive to continue with the horrible night. With the interior lights on, he saw that the blood had pooled on the floor of the front seat, and some of it had splattered on the dash during Gabe's coughing fits. Adam aimed the flashlight into the narrow areas of the dashboard. He was surprised at the amount of blood stuck in the tight spots.

The hot soapy water in the bucket looked like it was filled with red bubbles by the time he rinsed out the rags for the third time. Three fresh buckets of hot water later and some hard scrubbing and the job was almost done. After he was finished, it would take a forensics team to find any blood evidence in the car. He used clean rags to dab the carpet until it was almost dry. He threw the rags into the same trash bags that contained the license plates and registration.

Adam was glad for the unusual warm spell and rolled the windows down in hopes that the carpet would dry out soon. He placed a few large rocks in the bags to add weight. It would be best to let it disintegrate on the bottom of the lake for a while. He planned to get rid of the evidence first then go back for the women. As he dragged the bags out to the dock, he had to decide whether he was going to kill them in the cellar first and then drag them up the steps or have them walk out on their own at gunpoint. There wouldn't be any evidence if he killed them in the boat. That would be the best way. Before dumping them into the water, he would use the knife to open their lungs, like he did with Gabe.

At the water's edge, he threw the trash bags into the boat. He got in, rowed out a few yards, and tossed the bags over the side and into the deep. After that, it was time to get one of the women. Maybe he should get Sadie first. She would be the easy one.

All the interruptions had turned a simple night into

hours of work. Adam had no idea what time it was, but he knew it was late. It had to be close to dawn. He would have to hurry. After he was back at the dock, he got out of the boat and began to walk away when a bright light from the driveway of the next cabin over suddenly pierced the night. The glare of headlights lit the house's exterior. He heard two doors slam and then voices.

Damn, can this night get any worse?

He moved away from the boat, hoping no one saw him. He waited until the headlights went off then hurried to the cabin. He heard their conversation. A couple of men were talking about how good the fishing would be if they got a predawn start.

It seemed he would have to wait the rest of the night out. Nothing ever went right for him. He might as well just give it up, lie down, get some rest, and see what tomorrow night would bring. The moon would still be bright enough then. He'd be able to see what he was doing as he took the women out to the lake and dumped them. He didn't have to worry about going to work until Monday. No one was coming to visit Gabe. Adam went into the cabin, lay down on the couch, and fell asleep.

Chapter 30

Something cold and wet against his elbow caused Troy to wake up. He opened his eyes, lifted his head from the table, then realized he had dozed off and knocked over the glass of water sitting next to him. The pool of liquid expanded, getting close to his phone and laptop. Troy pushed away from the table. The bathroom was two steps from him, and he quickly jumped up to get a towel. After dabbing the table dry, he tipped his wrist to see the time—4:17 in the morning.

Did Eva call? Is Sadie okay?

He had been researching news clips from the armored car robbery that had happened close to Portland a few months ago. He grabbed his phone and checked the screen. No calls, nothing from Eva. He tapped her name and waited. The call went right to voicemail again. He felt helpless. How could he help his wife and sister when he had no clue where they were? It was infuriating. He knew Oliver and the kids must be asleep next door. They had been through a lot, and he wanted to let them get the rest they needed.

Troy put on his jacket, stuffed his phone in his pocket,

and left the motel room. He could use some coffee from the twenty-four-hour restaurant next door. He needed to get a buzz in his head and think of the next step. A booth by the window was open, so he took a seat and ordered coffee and the breakfast special.

He thought about his online search on the robbery. The exact amount of money taken from the armored truck heist was the same amount that those men had questioned Oliver about. That meant the cash hidden in the house had to be from that heist, and the renter, Lucas, had been involved. The cops had found one driver dead, and the other was in critical condition and in a coma at a Portland hospital. A minimum of two men had staged the robbery.

Evidence showed that the drivers had stopped in the middle of the road to move a fallen tree blocking their way. Since it was a small tree, they must have thought it would be easy for the two of them to move it off the road. After the robbery, investigators discovered that the tree had been purposely cut. It hadn't fallen from a recent storm or high winds. And $1,400,000 cash had been stolen from the truck. The only evidence from the getaway was the two sets of tire tracks found in the mud from ATV quads. They ran from the site of the heist through the woods and ended up at a side road a mile away, where they could easily have been ramped onto truck beds. Troy learned that .45-caliber bullets were removed from the deceased and from the wounded man. That was it. No other evidence was found, and there were no leads.

His phone rang. His hope that the call was from Eva

ended when he saw Mike's name on the screen. *Maybe he has some news.*

"Hey, Mike, find anything?"

"Forensics pulled a print from the refrigerator handle. They ran it through the county crime lab and checked it with AFIS. They got a hit. It's fresh and not from anyone in the family. You want to write this down?"

Troy took a pen and paper out of his shirt pocket. "Yeah, go ahead."

"The perp's name is Gabe Nolan. He did a six-month stint in the county jail for a convenience store robbery nine years ago. You can check him out on your laptop. It happened in the Portland area. He didn't use a weapon. He just took the cash and ran. That was why he got such a short sentence. Also, I looked over Sadie and Oliver's rental agreement with Lucas Castello. He went to school at Oakdale High in Portland. Never been married and doesn't have a criminal record. He's worked for himself as a freelance software writer for a Portland company, and we have no information that he ever worked for anyone else. Your family did a thorough job with the background check when they rented to him."

"Until we know where to go to find Sadie, and I hate to say it, Eva, I'll stay in the motel room and research both those guys. Since Lucas is dead, there has to be a third guy involved."

"I'm taking it that you haven't heard from Eva yet?"

Troy rubbed his forehead and took a deep breath. "No, Mike. I'm sure she's in trouble. She would never purposely lose contact with me. I just hope they're together and can help each other."

"The only other information I have is that Forensics removed the bullet from the kitchen wall and sent it to the county crime lab. They checked it for a ballistics match against the bullet that was taken from the deceased driver of the armored car heist. Just like we thought, it was a match. I wish I had better news for you. I'm going to stay in Albany, which is central to both Portland and Oliver and Sadie's house. At a minute's notice, I can go north, south, or east, where we last heard from Eva."

"Thanks, Mike. They must be holed up somewhere close by. The BOLO bulletin showed the last known location of the suspects to be in this area. The bad thing is that there are so many narrow country roads threading off Highway 20." Troy's voice cracked, and he cleared his throat. "I'll try to find a connection between those two and a third man."

They ended their call, and each promised to keep the other informed of any news. Troy took a couple of bites of his scrambled eggs and toast. The server came up to his table with a pot of hot coffee and refilled Troy's cup. He hoped that the research on Gabe's name would lead to an address or information about where he could be found. One more sip of coffee and Troy was ready to go to the motel and see what he could find on his laptop.

Once there, Troy pulled a chair up to the table in his room, sat down, and got to work. The first thing he wanted to find out was how Gabe and Lucas were connected. Gabe had served a few months in the county jail, but Lucas was clean. Troy had no idea what Gabe did for a living. Lucas was self-employed for a company called TechWare. That would be a good place to start. He typed the company's name in his search bar. They employed 8,700 people. TechWare was a major technology company in the Northwest and had opened its doors twenty-eight years ago. In one area of their website, users could type in an employee's name and pull up contact information. Troy decided to type in Lucas Castello's name first. There was a picture of him, and he had dark hair and a nice smile. Troy found no mention of his death. Apparently, they didn't update their site on a regular basis. Statistics revealed that he was a software developer for the company and had been employed with them for the last seventeen years. Next, Troy typed in Gabe Nolan, but nothing came up. He tried Gabriel Nolan. Nothing.

Let's try their high school.

A lot of schools were posting virtual yearbooks. It was the newest thing, and Troy hoped that Oakdale High would be one of them. He typed the name in the search bar and learned that the school was located on the east side of Portland. The website gave information about the staff and the history of the building—all details he wasn't interested in. Troy scrolled down to the middle of the web page. Bingo. There it was—the virtual yearbook. Troy felt a glimmer of hope.

The site let him register for free. He could search through the yearbook, but it said if he wanted a hardcover book, it would cost ninety-nine dollars and would take four to six weeks to arrive. That wasn't necessary. All he wanted was to see if there was a connection between the men. He made a calculated guess that Lucas had graduated between 2000 and 2003, since he was thirty-eight years old when he died, and he had been employed at TechWare for seventeen years. Troy typed in 2001 to give it a try. It was a lucky guess, and there he was. Lucas was a senior that year. Troy remembered that the seniors' yearbook pictures were always larger than those of the underclassmen.

Next was the big test, and Troy typed in Gabriel Nolan. His guess was right—the two were friends in high school, so that was the connection. Gabriel looked a little rough around the edges. Round-faced, no smile, brown hair, and carrying some extra weight.

So, this is the guy who shot at me.

Troy felt satisfied, positive that his return fire had connected with the bastard. He picked up his phone from the table and was about to call Mike when he saw the tab *Senior Activities and Extras*. Hoping to find out anything else that might be important, Troy clicked on it. He found images of senior dances, sports teams, and a lot of candid pictures of friends hugging, making body pyramids, and generally having fun. A tagline under some of the photos said things like *the most likely to succeed* and *will marry a lawyer and have ten kids*—crazy things. Troy scanned down to the last picture on the web page. Three guys had their arms around each other, laughing and goofing off. Troy recognized two of them, so he read the line below the photo. "Lucas, Gabe, and Adam, *most likely to become millionaires.*"

What? Adam? Could this be the third person?

The last names weren't printed under that picture. There was no question in Troy's mind that two of the men were Lucas and Gabe. He clicked on the web page back arrow until he got to all the formal senior photos. The second page of the section showed the smiling face of the same man who was in the candid shot—his full name was Adam Kent. The blood rushed to Troy's head, and his fingers clenched into fists.

He has my sister and probably my wife.

Chapter 31

"Do you hurt anywhere? What did he do to you?" Eva pulled the ropes away from her sister-in-law's ankles and wrists.

"He's crazy, a madman. I'm all right. Thank you for being here, for finding me. What about you? I saw him hit you with the branch and—oh my God, Eva, there's blood all over the side of your head."

"I'm okay. I was dizzy at first. It feels like it's only a surface wound. It's just a lot of blood. You're sure you're all right?"

"I don't physically hurt, except for the rope burns, but I hurt for my kids and Oliver. What is this guy doing? They found the money, so why did they have to take me?"

Eva rubbed Sadie's wrist for her and helped her sit up and lean against the wall. "There are a lot of people in this world who have lost their minds. They're so into having power and money that they have no compassion for others. Something snapped in their heads. I'm sorry to say that we're seeing it more and more every day. I wish you and your family didn't have to go through this, but I want you to know, we'll get out of here. Don't you worry."

Eva sat on the dirt floor with Sadie and looked around the room. She was surprised that the man had left the light on. He was probably so crazy that the thought of breaking the bulb hadn't entered his mind. He could have further traumatized them and left them in total darkness. Always preparing for the worst situation, Eva searched the cellar for items to help with their escape.

"Sadie, when was the last time you had something to eat?"

"I don't know. I guess on Christmas night, when you guys were there for dinner."

"There's a lot of canned goods here. I'll open a few jars, and we'll eat something while we figure out what to do next. Believe me, we're getting out of here. You need energy from food to be able to do that."

Eva checked out the shelves. They would start with pears then move on to green beans. She opened a couple of jars and sat against the wall. "You first." She gave one of the jars to Sadie.

Her sister-in-law stared at the jar of pears then began to cry. "How can I eat when I may never see my family again?"

Eva knew she had to be the strong one. "Your family is going to be very proud of you when they find out how you escaped from this maniac. Keep in mind, we're better than he is. We'll get out of here, and he'll either be dead or in prison for the rest of his life. You and your family will have a good life. Troy and I will visit you often. For right now, we have to eat, get our energy up, and think of a plan to get the hell out of here."

Sadie nodded, put her fingers in the jar, and ate the pear slices. Eva watched her and did the same. She had full confidence that they would escape, and she wanted Sadie to feel that way too. While Eva ate, she noticed the bottles on the shelves. A large wine rack sat next to the canned goods, and the bottles were angled downward to hold wine at the proper tilt. They could easily be broken, and the sharp ends would work as weapons. If the women were ready when he came down the stairs, each holding jagged glass on either side of the steps, they could take him by surprise, cut him, and get out of there. He could be the prisoner then. Eva told Sadie of her plan while handing her a jar of green beans and insisting she eat them.

Sadie was quiet, and Eva knew why, but she thought she would wait until Sadie admitted it.

"But what if I freeze up and can't go outside?"

Eva thought before she answered. She wasn't a psychologist, but she knew she had to respond in the correct way. "I'm not sure what to say. What if you imagined that Oliver, Willow, and Finn were waiting for you outside? Would that help you to go out there if you knew you could run to them?"

"I understand, logically, I do. That's what I'll focus on. My therapist always said to focus on what you want in life and that will help you to get it. Thank you. I'm sorry you had to go through all this, and I won't let you down. We'll get out of here, just like you said."

Eva's eyes pooled up with tears, but she quickly blinked and rubbed the wetness away from her cheek, not wanting to show any sign of weakness. She dipped her hand in the jar of green beans and took another bite. When she glanced at her sister-in-law, Eva was relieved to see that Sadie was eating and hopefully getting over her fears.

They needed to get ready. The bastard could open the door and come downstairs at any time. Eva walked to the rack of wine, grabbed two bottles by the neck, and slammed them against the shelf. She looked at the light bulb hanging from the ceiling. He would have his gun when he came down the steps. Sadly, he had her gun too. When they heard the metal lock slide away, she would throw something at the light and cause it to break. Then he would have to come down the steps blindly. She tried to imagine the details. He might have the flashlight with him. If so, that would mean both his hands would be holding something—the flashlight and the gun. She and Sadie would be on opposite sides of the last step. They would jab the broken glass into his neck just as his foot hit the cellar floor.

Then she heard it—the screeching and scraping of the metal lock.

Chapter 32

Troy had to calm down first before he called Mike. The name Adam Kent was probably common. He was sure there were at least a handful of them. Troy would Google that name in Portland, Oregon, and if nothing showed up as a possibility, he would expand his search throughout the state. If he came up empty, he'd check out social media next.

He went to Google's search engine and typed in *Adam Kent, Portland, Oregon.* He found eleven people with that name. Nothing looked interesting. He expanded his search to the state of Oregon, which had thirty-four entries. A middle name would've been helpful, but first and last was all he had. Troy clicked on each name, most having an image and age with it, but some didn't. He'd decided to look at two more entries then switch over to social media when he saw a clickable tag that said *Adam Kent Wins Bankers Award, Gold Mountain, Oregon.* Troy couldn't click on it fast enough. There he was, the same man, but wearing glasses and looking quite a bit older than he did in the high school yearbook photo. Gold Mountain was the town closest to where the armored car heist took place. Troy saved that information and forwarded it to Mike's email account then called him.

"I think I've got something," he said when Mike answered. "I sent you an email with the information in it. I found a connection between Gabe Nolan, Lucas Castello, and this guy named Adam Kent. I found them in the yearbook from Oakdale High. They were good friends, and all three were seniors. I did a Google search on Adam Kent and saw a man by that name who lives in Gold Mountain, Oregon, and get this, he won a banker's award. He worked at a bank, for God's sake."

"So he was the inside man getting the information to the other two."

"Can you call someone to get him hauled in for questioning?"

"Will do. Did you get an address on him?"

"No, he works at the Gold Mountain Federal Bank, though."

"The banks won't be open until Monday. They had a long weekend because of the Christmas holiday. Okay, I just pulled up the email. Yeah, I see his picture. I'll read the rest of the article and add that name to my address search along with Gabriel or Gabe Nolan. You do the same from your end. I'll issue a warrant on each of them to be brought in for questioning as soon as we know where to pick them up."

"Got it."

Troy pulled up a search engine for public records and started with Adam Kent. He typed in Gold Mountain for the city and Oregon for the state. Ten minutes later, he found an address, 382 Crest Acres Road, apartment 12, in

Gold Mountain. He called Mike to let him know.

"Great, I'll call for officers in that area to pick him up for questioning. I was just about to call you. I've got an address on Gabe. It's close, only about a half an hour from you. Take Highway 20 east and then north. This address also looks like an apartment, or maybe a duplex, 258 River End Road, number 2. It's in a small town called Baker Flats. This is getting out in the middle of nowhere. I'll call to see if I can get someone out there. In the meantime, I'm headed that way."

"I'll see you there."

Finally, an address to go to.

Troy tore off a piece of paper from the tablet on the table. He would write a note to Oliver and not leave him wondering where Troy had gone. After he wrote down the address of his and Mike's destination, he jotted down his cell phone number. No one had them memorized anymore, and Oliver might need to call him. The men had destroyed Oliver's phone, but Troy knew his brother-in-law would call from the motel office if needed. After he slipped the note under the adjoining door of the motel rooms, he grabbed a bottle of water and his gun, then he was out the door.

He quickly set his GPS for that address and was on the road. It was still dark out. The dawn's light was just beginning to glow over the mountain in front of him. He had the road to himself, which allowed him to exceed the speed limit and cautiously brake for curves.

Baker Flats. I've never heard of it.

Troy prayed that the women would be all right. Eva was strong, but Sadie was just beginning to get over her emotional problems. He couldn't wait to get his hands on the bastard who held them. Since Eva hadn't called him back, he knew that cell phone service would be questionable in that area. He hoped Mike was able to get an officer to the address right away. If not, Mike probably wasn't far behind him. When Troy saw the sign for the exit he needed, he turned off the highway and onto a narrow road, headed north.

He drove for twenty minutes as the road gradually climbed in elevation. After completing a hairpin curve, he saw the sign—*Baker Flats, Population 546*. Troy drove into the main part of town. Other than a few old houses, he saw only a mom-and-pop coffee shop, a grocery store, and a gas station. Two blocks up, a sign read River End Road, so he turned right and looked for the address that Mike had given him. There it was, 258. The house was old and run-down. A shop of some kind was on the first floor. A set of stairs on the side of the house went up to the second story. Troy took his Sig Sauer out from under the seat and tucked it behind his belt. It was early in the morning, and the town was quiet.

He looked in the window of the ground-floor shop before he walked to the stairs. It was a dusty old antique or junk store and didn't look inviting. He continued to the second story. The weight of each footstep caused the weathered boards to make a creaking sound. Troy rapped loudly on the door and waited. He pulled his jacket back and gripped his pistol, ready for whatever might happen. Nothing but silence. He knocked harder a second time.

"Y'all looking for Gabe?"

Troy heard a voice from the ground below and looked over the railing. An old man stood by an apple tree, pruning shears in his hands.

"Yes, I am. Does he live here?"

"Depends. Who's asking?"

Troy thought fast. "I'm a friend of his. My name is Troy. I used to go to school with him over at Oakdale High in Portland."

"Well, you should know, then, he ain't here. He spends most of his days at the cabin. Only comes back here a couple times a year."

Troy walked down the stairs to talk to the man at a closer range. "It's been so long since I've seen him. Your name is?" Troy reached out to shake the man's hand.

The old man obliged. "Most people call me Sam. That's good enough." He began to trim the twigs from the tree. He would snip, take a step back, then tilt his head and look at his accomplishment.

"Sam, can you tell me where the cabin is?"

"Yeah, it's over by Lost Lake somewhere. Can't say that I've ever been there, but the fishin's good. He always brings me back a nice catch, to eat fresh, and some more to put in the freezer."

"Do you live here?"

"About forty years now. I run the antique shop and live in the back."

Tires crunched on the gravel driveway and came to a sudden stop. Troy looked over his shoulder. Mike was there.

Good timing.

"The state trooper who just pulled up is my friend. We need to get into Gabe's apartment to get some information. I'll go over and talk to him for a minute, and then we'll both have some questions for you."

Troy hurried over to Mike. He told him that no one had answered the door, and the old man had said Gabe was at a cabin at a place called Lost Lake. Troy had no idea where it was located or how to get there. Mike typed it into his GPS, but nothing came up.

"Well, no results. Lost Lake's an appropriate name. Okay, let's question him some more and ask him to let us into the apartment. If he doesn't open it for us, we'll go in, anyway," Mike said.

They walked over to the old man. Mike introduced himself and asked the man if he was the landlord.

"Yeah, you might say that. I own the house, and Gabe gives me a few thousand dollars every year. He comes and goes as he pleases. Mostly goes."

"We need to get in contact with Gabe Nolan immediately. Someone's life may be in danger. If you don't know where his cabin is located, then we need to go inside to see if we can get information on its location."

Sam looked them over from head to toe and tipped his chin up. "Let's see the warrant."

Mike gave Troy a look of exasperation and said, "There's no time to get a warrant. We can legally go through the place under a law called exigent circumstances. Feel free to look it up. You can open the door for us now with the key, or we can break it down."

"Okay, okay, don't get your pants up in a wad. I'll go get the key." The old guy walked to the door of his antique shop and went inside.

Mike told Troy that the mountains surrounding them were full of small lakes and country roads, but he had never heard of Lost Lake.

"I've never heard of it either," Troy said. "This is the only address that came up as his, so we have to hope we'll find something in the apartment that will show us where it is."

Sam came back with a key ring crammed with keys. He looked down at it as he flipped one key after another.

"Here we go. I think this is it." He held one of the keys up in the air. He grabbed hold of the handrail and slowly walked up the rickety stairs. Troy and Mike followed.

Chapter 33

Sam put the key in the lock and turned it. He pushed his hand against the door as it slowly opened with a creak. When he followed the old man and Mike inside, Troy noticed the musty odor that permeated the room. Although it was winter, it was an unusually warm day. Sam walked to the living room window and opened it.

"There you go." He turned around and faced them. "Gabe hasn't been here for a few months, and we need fresh air in here."

"Does he ever have visitors, friends, or relatives?" Troy asked.

"Can't say that he does, at least not that I've ever seen. He talked about a brother that he had who lived up in Washington. He died a while back, a couple years ago. Gabe used to meet up at the cabin with his brother and some of his buddies on his fishing trips."

Troy walked to the small desk in the corner of the room and opened the top drawer. It was stuffed full of papers, and he had to pull hard on the knob to get it open. "And his brother's name was?"

"Don't know that he ever said. I think he just called him his brother."

"Well, thanks for opening the door. We'll let you know when we're finished," Mike told Sam as he walked over to the cluttered kitchen table. He began to go through the papers stacked there.

"Yeah, I'll be outside working on pruning that tree. Holler down if you have any questions."

Troy and Mike continued to go through various stacks of papers and junk that littered almost every corner of the room. They were hoping to find an address or clue about where the cabin or Lost Lake was.

"I typed it in my phone's GPS app, too, and nothing came up. I wonder if it's officially named or if the locals just call it that. If we don't find a clue soon, we could ask around at the grocery store and gas station," Troy said.

"Yeah, that's an idea," Mike agreed. "There's a few pictures here. It looks like these were taken at a lake. I don't see anything in the background, though, besides water. Here's one of Gabe holding up a stringer of fish. Someone had to take this picture." He flipped it over. "It looks like an old one, back when the photo labs actually printed the date that the picture was developed. This one was taken six years ago."

"I'll check out the bedroom and see if there's anything in there," Troy said as he left the living room. A framed picture sat on top of the dresser. Troy walked over, picked it up, and studied it. The horizontal double frame held two five-by-seven photos. The picture on the left was of Gabe, Adam, and Lucas, the three high school buddies—the three who were involved in the heist and the three who were responsible for Sadie and Eva's disappearance. The picture on the right was of a cabin. Water was in the foreground, so the photo had to have been taken from a boat in the lake. Troy looked closer at the mountains behind the cabin. A cell phone tower stood at the top of one mountain. He could hardly make it out, but he knew it wasn't a bare tree. It was clearly a cell tower. He hurried to the living room, where Mike was still going through stacks of papers.

"Check this out." He showed the framed five by sevens to Mike. "Look closely at the top of that mountain. It's a cell phone tower. Isn't there an online map of tower locations?"

"There sure as hell is. Not positive if the signal could reach the cabin, though. Too many hills up close to it that could block it out. Let's take this along and check out the maps on our laptops. We could stop at the store and gas station on the way out of town to see if anyone knows where this lake is. Once we locate the tower, we can Google Map it in satellite view to find the lakes and roads in the area."

Troy turned the frame over, removed the backs, and slid the pictures out. Then he and Mike left the apartment. On the way down the steps, they saw Sam still pruning the tree. Troy showed the photos to him and asked if the lake or mountains or the two other men beside Gabe looked familiar.

"No, those mountains look like all the other mountains around here. And the same with the lake. Sorry, can't help you."

"Thanks, we're finished for now. We'll let you know if we need to get back in," Troy said as he hurried to his car.

They both got into their vehicles and turned on the laptops to begin a search for cell tower maps. Mike got the information first and walked over to Troy's car. Troy rolled down the window as he waited for a map to appear on his screen.

"It looks like there's one on a mountain approximately fifty miles away from here. The screen shows the roads to get there. Some of them look like logging roads," Mike said.

"Okay, I've got the same screen up. I see what you mean. When I click out to get more of a view, I see a lot of lakes in the area. Most are unnamed."

"Yeah, that's our problem. Let's head that way but first fill up at the gas station on our way out of town. We can show the attendant the picture and see if they have knowledge of the lake's location."

Troy arrived at the gas station first. While the attendant filled his Jeep with fuel, he got out of his car and showed him the picture.

"Excuse me. I'm trying to find this lake. People are calling it Lost Lake, but I don't see it on any GPS maps. Do you know where it is? Can you tell by its surroundings?"

The attendant looked at the picture for a minute then shook his head. "No, it doesn't look familiar, sorry."

Mike pulled up behind Troy, who walked over to his window and said, "The attendant here isn't familiar with this lake. It looks like the grocery store across the street isn't open. I'll drive over to the café to ask and meet you there."

"Got it."

A three-block drive down the main street and Troy pulled into the parking lot at the café. Almost all the spaces were taken. For a small café, it was full of patrons. Troy walked in and stood at the counter. A middle-aged woman holding a coffeepot hollered over to him.

"Sorry, a seat should be opening up soon," she said, as she refilled a man's cup.

Troy held up the picture of the lakeside cabin and showed it to her. "I see you're very busy, but I just have a quick question. Would you happen to know where this cabin is, or the lake, based on its surroundings? Some people call it Lost Lake. It's important. Two people may be in danger there."

"In danger? I don't like to hear that. I can't tell you where it is, but I can tell you that half of these people in here are headed for mountain lakes as soon as they're done eating. I'll see what I can do." She took the picture from Troy's hand and walked around the café tables, talking to some of the patrons. Troy watched as people put their glasses on, looked closer at the picture, and shook their heads.

Despair was coming over him. Troy's stomach churned.

Now what? Drive around until we stumble upon it? Get a helicopter?

As the woman began to walk toward Troy, a man sitting at a table that she had just passed told her to stop.

"Let me see that again. Yeah, that's it." He squinted and looked closer. He reached in his shirt pocket, pulled out his glasses, and put them on. "That's Lost Lake. I thought something in that picture looked familiar. That's Gabe's cabin. I was just out there last summer renting a house across the lake from it."

Troy was elated. "Can you tell me how to get there? It's important. There are people whose lives are in danger who could be held there."

"If you're asking me what roads to take and turn off onto, then no. If lives are in danger, then I suggest you follow me, or I could ride with you and show you. It's a long way out to the place, but I have nothing better to do."

Troy knew that following him would take a lot more time than if he invited the man to ride with him.

"Please, come with me. We have a state trooper who'll follow us."

Chapter 34

Adam awoke to the sound of birds chirping in their evensong. It took him a minute to realize where he was and what he was about to do.

Oh yeah, it's time to kill the women and dump their bodies in the lake.

It wasn't a pleasant thought, but it was a necessary evil. If he wanted to escape the mundane life he had been in for years, there were steps he needed to take. He had to pat himself on the back. So far, not only had he thought of an excellent plan, but it had also worked. A few unexpected situations had happened. Both of his friends were dead. He had to remember that he was the one who would get to keep over a million dollars all to himself.

To the victor go the spoils.

He pulled himself off the couch and walked to the window to look at the house next door. The boat was back in the driveway. He guessed the guys were through fishing for the day. A couple of lights were still on. Not knowing how long they planned on staying there, he needed to get his tasks done that night and get home. He'd wait another hour or so, until the neighbors' lights went out, then go get the women.

His stomach growled. Adam went to the refrigerator and pulled the door open. There wasn't much in there, and he could tell Gabe hadn't bought groceries in a while. He took out a plate of leftover fish, smelled it, and put it back. He looked in the cupboard, saw a can of soup, opened it, and dumped it in a pan. As he stirred and the soup simmered, he thought the situation over and decided he would get everything done as soon as he finished eating. He hadn't taken his gloves off in a couple of days, and they were bothering him. He tried to ignore the feeling and remember that by wearing them, his fingerprints wouldn't be left behind. When he was hired at the bank, his prints were taken and stored in the system. He had to think of every detail. Doing time in prison was not an option. Neither was living from paycheck to paycheck.

He sat at the table in the dark and looked out at the house next door. As he watched, two men paced in front of the window of a well-lit room. After his last bite, he saw the lights go off and the men exit out the back door. They threw a couple of duffel bags into the back seat of the truck and drove away. He was alone on the lake again. No witnesses.

Time to get this done.

On his way to the cellar, he pulled the gun out of his pocket, ready to shoot if the women didn't cooperate. He slid the metal bar out of the hasp and opened the door. His foot was on the first step when the light hanging from the ceiling shattered. Everything went dark.

What are they up to?

His gun was ready, but the flashlight was on the kitchen table. They'd shattered the light on purpose. That, he knew. They were waiting to surprise him in some morbid way. He wouldn't let their tricks mess him up again. He stepped back up, climbed out, and locked the door again before returning to the kitchen for the flashlight. Walking back, he thought things over and decided to take Sadie out first. She would be easy to kill. He'd save the feisty one for later. He'd get Sadie out of the cellar at gunpoint, shoot her when she was in the boat, and leave no evidence. Later, he would do the same to the other woman.

He was ready for whatever they had in store for him. He walked to the cellar, turned on the flashlight, and opened the door. He shined it around the shelves. They must be hiding, since he didn't see them anywhere. He took a couple of steps down and shined the light around the room. They were probably at the far wall, hiding behind the shelves.

"Hey, you two, I know where you're hiding. Give it up. Make it easier on yourself. I'm just going to take you on a little boat ride. Nothing to worry about, especially if you can swim. If I don't get your cooperation, I can shoot you right down here. I'd rather not, though. More blood to clean up."

He walked down a few more steps and flashed the light on the back wall and around the shelves. "Ladies, I'm talking to you. Show yourselves now. I'm giving you a chance to survive."

Adam put his foot on the last step, trained his light on the end of the shelves, and pointed his gun. Pain came suddenly to both sides of his body. Sharp objects pierced his skin. He dropped the flashlight and brought his hand up against his neck. When he drew it back, blood covered the palm of his hand. "Damn you!"

The ambush took him by surprise. He turned to his right and saw the silhouette of one of the women holding up a broken bottle, ready to bring it down on him again. Adam steadied his pistol and pulled the trigger.

Chapter 35

The sound of the blast was deafening as it echoed throughout the small cellar. For a split second, the light from the explosion of the gun brightened the room. Sadie saw the look of surprise and pain in Eva's face as she fell to the ground. Adam's foot caught on the last step after they cut him. He tripped and lay on the dirt next to her. When he loosened his grip, the pistol fell from his hand. Sadie sprinted for the gun, but Adam rolled to his side, reached out, and grabbed it before she could intercept it. She didn't have a chance, and there was no way she could hit him with the bottle again or grab the gun. If there was any hope at all of saving Eva's life and her own, she had to leave. Sadie ran for the steps.

The boom from the second shot caused her to wince, and she waited for pain that didn't come.

He missed.

Sadie reached the top of the steps, leaving the confinement of the manmade crypt and entering the twilight of the evening. She ran for the nearest tree and stood behind it, trying to decide where to go next.

The man emerged from the cellar and screamed into the

night, "I'll kill you, too, you bitch." His arm was extended, holding the gun and ready to shoot. He was searching for her.

Where can I go?

Sadie had to get help but hated to leave Eva. She choked back a scream of terror and hopelessness as she prayed that Eva was still alive. Eva had risked her life for her, and Sadie knew she had to do the same in return. Her mind was spinning. Hoping to find a landline phone at one of the houses around the lake, she decided to run to the closest one. Adam couldn't see her among the dense trees, so she was safe for the moment.

The house was a few hundred yards away and didn't look occupied. She was still barefoot, and her feet were almost numb. She tried to avoid stepping on the sharp rocks as she ran. When she got to the house, she tried the knob on the front door. As expected, it was locked, and she would have to break in through a window. One of the large rocks in the landscaping served as her tool. After picking it up, she hurried to the side of the house. The window was tall and low to the floor. It looked like the living room might be behind it. She peered in and saw that it would be easy to get in once the window was broken. She would have to be cautious of sharp glass and make sure she didn't cut herself.

Sadie stood back about six feet and hurled the rock against the window. The crash was loud. She hoped it would set off an alarm but no luck. A small outdoor rug lay on the patio. She grabbed it and threw it on the floor inside the room. It was easy to bring her leg over the window frame and put her foot down firmly on the rug. When she brought her other leg over, a jagged piece of glass pierced her thigh, and she stifled a scream. Once inside, she cased the room, lit only by moonlight coming in the windows. She didn't want to risk giving away her position by turning on a light. Quickly, she looked around the living room, and it lacked a phone. She ran to the kitchen, hoping to see one hanging on the wall, like everyone had before cell phones.

Dammit, no landline phones anymore.

She hurried to the bedroom to see if a phone was on a nightstand. Nothing. She opened the closet, grabbed a sweatshirt and pants, and got dressed. The shoes were too big for her, but they would protect her feet and help her run faster. Back in the living room, she went to the window and looked toward the cabin. There he was, holding his hand against his neck and making his way to the house she was standing in.

How far is the next house?

She had to leave. Getting to a phone was the only thing that would save their lives. On her way out the back door, she picked up a flashlight that she saw lying on a bench and grabbed a jacket from a coatrack before she fled into the woods. If she followed the path around the lake, she had a chance of coming across another house. Fearing he would see the light from the flashlight, she put it in her jacket pocket for later. She would follow the moonlight that reflected on the edge of the water.

How far behind me is he? Can he see me?

Questions filled her mind as she ran. Stones and branches

obstructed her path as she tried to run over them without tripping. She was out of breath and had to stop for a moment. Sheltering behind a tree, she looked back at the path to see whether he was following. She was safe for the moment. After catching her breath, she continued on.

Off in the distance was the silhouette of an A-frame cabin. That was where she would go. If they didn't have a phone, she would head for the mountain road and hope a car would come by.

Sadie ran, got to the A-frame, and took the walkway to the back of the house. A few steps up to the deck and she was at a sliding glass door. She remembered that Oliver would always forget to lock the sliding door to the balcony at their high-rise apartment in Seattle. She would tell him that it was important and he needed to remember. He would laugh and ask her who could climb up the side of the building and crawl in, Spiderman? She had to smile just thinking of him saying that. Tears welled up in her eyes in disbelief at everything that was happening. She had to get through the nightmare and get back to them, and Eva had to be all right.

She grabbed the slider's handle and pulled to the side—it opened. Relief flooded through her. She stepped inside, locked the door behind her, and searched the house. There wasn't a phone downstairs, so she ran up to the second floor. The first bedroom didn't have one, so she ran to the second. Sadie couldn't believe her eyes when she spotted an old-fashioned landline phone on the nightstand. Her heart nearly jumped into her throat as she picked it up and dialed 911.

"Nine-one-one, what is your emergency?"

"I need help. A man is trying to kill me, and he may have already killed my friend."

"What is the address?"

"I don't know. I'm at a lake, and I broke into someone's cabin to find a phone. He's coming after me."

"Okay, ma'am, stay on the phone, please. We're tracing your call. Do you know—" The phone went dead.

"Hello, hello. Are you there?" Sadie pushed the receiver's button over and over again.

It can't be. Could he have cut the line? Why would the phone be dead?

She had to get out of there. In every horror movie she had ever seen, the dumb people were trapped upstairs. Looking around for a weapon, she found a heavy brass vase on the bedroom dresser. That would be better than nothing. Sadie picked it up and cautiously walked to the stairs. Too late—footsteps were coming up from the first floor. She tiptoed back into the bedroom and hid behind the opened door. She could hear him as he got to the top step and walked down the hall into the first bedroom. A few seconds later, he was in the hall again, walking to the room where she hid. Sadie held up the vase and prepared to bring it down hard on his head when he entered. She heard his footsteps. They stopped right outside the bedroom door. He took a couple of steps inside, then she saw his head and swung hard.

Chapter 36

Adam was furious. She'd hit him on the head with something, and the blinding pain had caused him to drop to his knees.

What the hell did she do? Why is she so hard to kill?

When he opened his eyes, he saw her legs as she ran out of the room. His finger was still on the trigger, and he shot three times. There was no sound of a fall or a scream. He'd missed.

Then he heard her footsteps on the kitchen floor as she left. Adam couldn't take it anymore. He threw back his head and screamed.

His neck throbbed from the glass shards the women had pierced him with. He was afraid he was losing too much blood. He had to get out of there, so Adam grasped the doorknob to steady himself and pulled up on his feet. He staggered to the stairs, grabbed the handrail, and made his way down to the first floor. His gun was ready in case he saw her again. His goal was to make it to his car and get the hell home. He could nurse his wounds and continue with his plan. Adam got out onto the deck and down the steps then continued along the lake's edge as he painfully walked to his car.

He considered the situation. He could still get away with all of this. The women never really saw his face in any light. The one was probably dead, and the other one was just crazy. He'd worn gloves throughout the last couple of days. He was careful in Sadie and Oliver's house, Gabe's cabin, and the woman's car when he drove it behind the garage. All evidence had been dumped in the lake. Blood evidence was the only trace of him left behind. His DNA wasn't on file anywhere. Just to be safe, he would drive home while it was still dark and stash the money somewhere away from his apartment until he was ready to leave the country. The cops had to know by then that the hidden money was from the armored car robbery. He'd mistakenly asked Oliver where the one million four hundred thousand was. That was his first mistake. He shouldn't have mentioned the amount. The FBI might search the homes of bank employees. He was surprised they hadn't already done that. They'd been questioned at work, but no employees that he knew of had had their homes checked. When he went back to work on Monday, he could keep a winter scarf draped around his neck to hide the cuts. If anyone asked, he could say he was fighting off a cold.

Finally, he was at his car. He looked around. He didn't see the woman and didn't care about her anymore. He just wanted to get home. He checked the back of the car to make sure the two duffel bags were still there, started the ignition, and drove away from Gabe's cabin.

His blinding headache was getting worse. He still had a few hours before he would be home, and he just wanted to sleep. That couldn't happen—he had to stay awake. He rolled down the window to get the cold air coming in on his face. Then he turned on the radio. He needed something loud, so rock 'n roll would do. Adam continued to plan.

Attention to detail. The smallest item overlooked can ruin everything.

The small town of Moonstone was coming up at the next exit. A large coffee and hamburger were just what he needed. He pulled off the road to go through the drive-in. After barking his order into the menu sign, he glanced at himself in the mirror. He looked terrible. He pulled up his collar to hide the cuts. He had a comb in the glove compartment, and he took it out and ran it through his hair before it was his turn at the window.

"A large black coffee and a double cheeseburger."

"Would you like fries with that?"

"Yeah, go ahead. Would you include a cup of water and extra napkins?"

"Sure, that'll be six forty-nine. Please drive forward to the next window."

He thought it strangely obscene that life went on with people saying everyday phrases like "Would you like fries with that?" It was ludicrous that a normal routine continued after all that had happened in the last two days.

Adam pulled over and parked, poured water on the napkins, washed his face and hands, then pulled down the vanity mirror to check his reflection. He wet more napkins and blotted the blood on his neck. Then he peeled the paper back from his double cheeseburger and took a bite.

He didn't have much farther to go and was getting close to Gold Mountain. He needed to decide where to stash the two duffel bags. It had to be somewhere away from everyone's eyes, somewhere that he could get in and out without being seen. He thought about the large cement culvert a couple of miles from his apartment, out in the country. It was always dry, even in the winter. The bags would be safe in there. The spot was elevated and next to a deep ditch that no one in their right mind would walk in. He remembered seeing it because it looked so odd, like an engineering mistake.

Perfect, problem solved. He could have the hood of his car opened just in case someone went by and wondered why he was parked there. He could say the engine was acting up.

Adam turned the radio up a little louder and stepped on the gas, eager to get the night over with. Finally, when he realized he was getting close to that area, he slowed down and watched for the exact spot.

There it is.

He pulled over and parked. After grabbing the flashlight, he walked to the front of the Denali and raised the hood. He looked up and down the long, dark road. No headlights were coming from either way as far as he could see. He shined the light over at the culvert. It was just like he remembered, high and dry. He turned the flashlight down at the bottom of the ditch. There was no water in it. He remembered that the weather was predicted to be dry for the next few days.

He walked to the back of the car and opened the hatch. After grabbing a bag in each hand, he lifted them out and climbed into the ditch. He held the flashlight in his armpit. With its beam, he saw that the culvert was completely empty. No sticks, branches, or dead animals were there. He pushed the duffel bags in, walked away, and drove home.

Fifteen minutes later, Adam was in his apartment. He walked into the bedroom and crawled into bed.

Chapter 37

They had been driving on the narrow winding road for fifteen minutes when Troy realized he hadn't asked the guy his name. "I'm sorry. My name is Troy Winters, and the trooper who's following us is Sergeant Mike Stevens. I don't think I've asked you your name."

"Oh, that's right. I'm Zachary Palermo. Just call me Zak."

"Zak, you don't know how much I appreciate the fact that you offered to come with us. Before you did, all we had were terrain maps showing unnamed landmarks and people telling us that it's out there somewhere. I don't know if we would've found it, otherwise. Thanks for offering to show us."

"Well, I sure hope my memory serves me correctly. But I've always been pretty good with my sense of direction. If someone's in danger, I want to do everything I can to help. Besides, I'm retired and bored. Can you tell me what's going on up there that you're concerned about?"

Troy continued to drive uphill as he took the curves carefully. He was averaging only twenty-five miles an hour.

"We have reason to believe that my sister and my wife are being held by two men out there. We think one of them is Gabe."

"Gabe? You mean the guy who owns the cabin?"

"Yes, what do you know about him?"

Zak shuffled in his seat, pulled out a handkerchief, and blew his nose. "Like I said, it was a year ago when I rented the cabin. Me and a couple guys were out on our boat fishing when Gabe hollered over from his boat and asked how we were doing. What kind of luck were we having, he asked us. At the time, we were doing pretty good, reeling in the bass. Long story short, he wasn't having much luck that day. We told him where we were staying and invited him over for a fish fry."

Troy glanced at Zak. "What kind of guy was he?"

"He just seemed like a regular guy to me. Kind of loud and obnoxious like some guys are. Can't think of anything else to tell you about him. That's the only time I saw him, and he told us that the cabin across the lake was his."

They drove along in silence for a few minutes, and Zak told him to slow down, saying he thought the next place to turn was coming up. He said it was right after the tall Douglas fir tree that was dead.

"We're not positive that they're held up there, but we have reason to believe it. I don't know what to expect when we arrive. You'll need to be ready for anything."

"Don't worry about me. I just hope everyone's all right. Keep in mind, I'll be ready to help if needed."

Troy's phone rang. It was Mike. "Hey, what's up?"

"I'm glad we have that guy showing us the way," Mike told him.

Troy touched the speaker app so everyone could hear the conversation. "Me too. I've got you on Speaker. By the way, his name is Zak, he's got a good sense of direction, and he's ready to help us with whatever we need."

"Couldn't ask for more. Zak, can you guess how much longer until we get there? I'm just wondering if you'll have trouble finding the way after dark."

"Oh yeah, it'll probably be dark. We still have an hour or so. I think I'll be fine, though. The last part is one long, straight stretch. We got another turn coming up. Take a left at the next road."

"Great. Okay, I'll be right behind you. Later."

"So if you don't mind me asking, how did this all come about? How did it happen that Gabe and another man might be holding your wife and sister? A hostage or kidnapping situation?" Zak asked.

Troy took a deep breath. "Yes. We have reason to believe that there was robbery money hidden in my sister's house. Her name is Sadie. She was taken hostage, and my wife, Eva, was trying to find her when she went missing too. At least, she hasn't called or answered her phone. That's not like her at all. She would be in touch if everything was all right."

"So sorry to hear that."

Troy turned on the headlights and shifted in his seat. "We think that Gabe and a man named Adam are together. I shot and wounded one of them. Do you remember what kind of physique Gabe has?"

"Shorter than average and heavyset."

"That could have been him. Sounds like the one who caught my bullet."

They continued on in silence. Troy was anxious to get there and hoped both women would be unharmed and the nightmare would end.

"This should be the last turn, right up here. After that, we'll go straight for a few minutes, and then we'll be at the road to the lake."

Troy made the turn and stepped hard on the gas for the last stretch. Mike was close behind.

"Okay, here it is. Turn right. We should be able to see the lake anytime now. Gabe's cabin is at the first driveway we come to."

Troy slowed down to make the turn. The lake was visible in the moonlit night. The driveway to the cabin was coming up. Then he slammed on his brakes. Mike swerved to miss rear-ending him. The Jeep's headlights caught a woman running toward them, her hands waving in the air.

Oh my God, it's Sadie.

Chapter 38

Troy got out of the car and ran to her. "Sadie! My God, are you all right?" He saw her legs begin to buckle, and he put his arms around her so she wouldn't fall.

"Thank God, you're here." Her voice was weak. "I'll be okay. It's Eva. We have to get to her."

Mike's car door slammed as he got out and ran to them. "Sadie, where is the man who took you?"

"I saw him leave in his car. I think the other guy's dead. Help me get to the cabin. Eva's in the cellar. It's over there on the other side of the garage."

Mike hung on to her while Troy took off running toward the garage. He ran to the back and saw the cellar door.

"Eva, I'm here!" he screamed while sliding the metal bar out of the hasp. He pushed the door aside and looked down into the dark hole. He hollered back to Zak and Mike, "Someone, grab a flashlight! Hurry. Where are you, babe?" He continued to walk down to Eva, carefully finding each step with his foot and hanging on to the handrail.

The cellar floor lit up. Zak was behind him with the

flashlight. He stood at the top of the stairs and moved the light until they saw her.

"Eva!" Troy ran to her side. Her face was ghostly white, and blood covered her chest and dripped down the side of her face. Troy gently put his hand behind her neck, lifted her head, and put his ear to her mouth. She was breathing.

"Troy." Her voice came out in a whisper as she opened her eyes slightly. "You're… here."

Troy looked up at the door, and Mike had just walked up with Sadie. He peered into the cellar and asked if she was okay.

"She's been shot. Radio for a rescue helicopter. Hurry."

Mike helped Sadie steady herself and stand next to Zak, then he ran off to call for help.

"Babe, we'll get you out of here. Where are you hurting?"

"My chest… hurts… and the side of my face burns," she said.

He checked out her side and saw the area the bullet had entered. He felt her back for an exit wound and found it, along with a shattered rib. Troy gently let her head back down while he took off his jacket and wrapped it around her for warmth. He kept the sleeve pressed against the exit wound to prevent further blood loss. She had to stay warm.

Troy kissed her on the forehead and let her know that help was on the way. "I love you, Eva. I'm so sorry this happened."

"Sadie's okay, right?"

"She is, thanks to you."

Mike appeared at the opening and hollered down. "A

copter is on its way. ETA is twenty-five minutes."

Troy yelled up, "Mike, come down here! We need to get Eva out and be ready to be transferred."

Mike joined them at the bottom of the steps.

"We're going to get you out of this cellar," Troy told his wife.

"Yes."

"We'll move you slowly, honey. Tell us if it hurts too much. Mike and I will get on either side of you and help you stand. We'll move gently. Tell us if it hurts too much."

"Okay."

They helped her to her feet, and slowly, all three took small steps. When they got to the narrow staircase, Mike stepped behind her, guiding her forward.

Sadie hurried to Eva's side. They all walked to the clearing and waited for the helicopter.

"I've notified police and a forensics unit. I'm sure the FBI will be engaged in this, too, since federal money is involved," Mike told Troy. "I'll wait for them here."

"Okay, Mike, thanks. Zak, you don't know how much I've appreciated your help. I'm going to go with my wife and sister on the flight to the hospital. Could I get you to take my car back to Baker Flats? I'll meet up with you in a couple days. The keys are in it. Just leave your phone number with Mike."

"Sure, I'll do that. I hope they'll both be all right."

The sound of the approaching Emergency Medical Services helicopter gave Troy an overwhelming sense of relief.

They'll be okay.

As soon as it landed in the clearing, the paramedics ran out with a stretcher. While they helped Eva onto the stretcher and into the EMS helicopter, they asked Troy what he knew about her injuries.

Troy had his arm around Sadie, ready to walk with her to board. The noise was deafening. He turned to Mike and yelled, "Mike, my Sig Sauer is under the front seat of my Jeep! Will you get it and keep it with you?"

"Of course. I'll talk to you soon. Let me know how they both are when you can."

One of the EMTs reached out and helped them climb aboard. Troy took a seat close to Eva and held her hand. Sadie sat by his side.

The upward wobble of the helicopter made Troy lightheaded as they floated away.

Chapter 39

Troy held Eva's hand until they arrived at the hospital in Portland twenty minutes later. After they landed, a gurney was rushed out to the helicopter. Troy watched as the medical staff raised the gurney's platform to adjust to the level of the door's opening. Eva was easily transferred and whisked off to the emergency room. A wheelchair was brought out for Sadie, and just as quickly, she was taken away too.

Troy provided the necessary medical information at the front desk, the last step before he could contact Oliver. After he answered all the questions, he looked up the phone number for the motel they were staying at along Highway 20 and called the front desk. Troy explained that the man in 4A didn't have a phone and that it was important that he speak to him. The clerk said he would go to the room and get Oliver. He put Troy on hold.

Troy heard Willow's voice before Oliver had a chance to say hello. "Is it Mom? Is she okay?" Almost at the same time, little Finn yelled, "Can I talk to Mommy? I miss her."

Troy gave a prayer of thanks, knowing he could tell them that she was fine.

"Hello, Troy? Has she been found?"

"I'm so happy to tell you that Sadie's safe. She's bruised and shaken, but she's okay."

"Oh, thank God, Troy. We've been so worried. Where are you?"

"I'm at the Portland hospital. Sadie's getting first aid and being checked for anything more serious. Eva was shot but conscious when we found her. She's in the emergency room right now, and I'm waiting to hear from the doctor."

"What? Oh no, I'm so sorry to hear that. I pray that she'll be okay. What happened?"

"It's a long story. I'll tell you everything when I see you. Go ahead and rent a car and come up here. Plan on staying at our downtown apartment for a while."

"We'll do that. I'll see you at the hospital in a couple of hours."

"I'll be here."

"And Troy, thanks."

Troy went downstairs to the café and bought a large coffee. He took it back up with him and sat down on a comfortable couch in the waiting room. He leaned back and closed his eyes. The worst was over. He prayed for Eva's recovery. He had seen many gunshot wounds in his line of work. Her wounds were serious, but hopefully, the bullet hadn't hit any major organs. It was his fourth time of feeling the bullet, Eva's first. In the past, he had been shot once in his right thigh, once on his right side that just grazed his ribs, and each shoulder had taken a bullet, the latest just yesterday. The shot to the ribs was the worst. He knew Eva had been hit in the ribs, too, and that she would have a long, uncomfortable time until she recovered. He cherished his eleven years of marriage to his beautiful, smart, and courageous wife. He could never lose her.

That familiar pain burned in his shoulder, reminding him that his most recent wound hadn't been looked at yet. With all the worry over Eva and Sadie, he had forgotten about it. He promised himself that after he learned about Eva's condition, he would get the wound cleaned and bandaged properly. He had to make sure it didn't get infected.

Troy watched as people in the waiting room came and went. Some were happy and hugging, telling each other whether the baby was a boy or a girl. Some were crying and had to leave when they got their news. Everyone was in their own world.

A doctor walked in. "Troy Winters?"

He jumped up. "Yes, that's me."

"Hello, I'm Dr. Norris. Well, the good news is that the bullet that hit your wife exited her body and missed vital organs. Her wounds are cleaned, and we're monitoring for internal bleeding. We're considering surgery since two ribs were badly fractured. We may use a rib-plating technique to help her stabilize and heal faster. A bullet grazed her cheekbone. The wound is cleaned and bandaged. She'll have a large scar there and may choose to have cosmetic surgery in the near future. As of right now, I just wanted to let you know she will live. She'll need to be hospitalized for a couple of days, three to four at the most. I would predict a complete recovery in six weeks or so, depending on how she practices her therapy."

"Thank you, Doctor. When can I see her?"

"She's on pain medication and is resting peacefully. I would wait until tomorrow morning if I were you. Rest is necessary and aids in healing."

"I'll do that. Thank you."

As soon as the doctor walked away, Sadie was wheeled out to the waiting room.

"Sadie, I'm so glad to see you. How are you feeling?"

"I'm okay, really." She thanked the nurse and stood up, bracing herself against Troy's arm as he led her to a chair. "How's Eva? That's who I'm worried about."

"She's doing okay and will recover just fine. I talked to her doctor. She's stabilized and may need surgery, but she's sleeping right now. We can see her in the morning."

"Thank God. I need to call Oliver and the kids. Are they okay?"

"Yes, I called them a while ago. They've rented a car and should be here within an hour. Let's go to the café. I'll buy you dinner, sister."

They sat down at a corner booth. The server greeted them and poured cups of coffee. They each ordered a comforting bowl of beef stew with a side of buttermilk biscuits.

While Troy stirred the cream into his coffee, he asked Sadie if she wanted to talk about the details of what happened after she was taken away.

She took a deep breath, exhaled slowly, and began. "I'm not sure why they took me. They had already found the money.

When they forced me away from the kids, well, that was the hardest part. I was still blindfolded, and my legs and hands were tied when they put me in the back seat. One man was shot as he was getting into the passenger side, but I can only go on the sounds I heard. I heard the driver call him Gabe. That was you that shot him, wasn't it? And you're wounded too?"

"Yes, to both questions. I just wish I could have stopped them right there. Don't worry about me, though. The bullet didn't hit a bone, and I'm going to have it looked at soon. I'm in the right place for that." He smiled at her.

Before she continued with her story, she reached across the table and rubbed the top of her brother's hand. "The men were talking about the pain and all the blood. I was yelling at them and trying to convince them to let me go. The one who was shot, Gabe, got quiet after a while. The driver pulled over and, from what I could hear, got sick on the side of the road. He drove for a couple of hours and then came to a final stop. He pulled Gabe's body out of the car. Just a few minutes later, Eva was there untying me. How did she know where to find me?"

Troy took a sip of his coffee before answering. "We had you tracked through the GPS in Willow's watch until the battery went dead. She found you by pure luck after that."

"What? Oh my God, Troy. I forgot about the GPS. You got the text she sent you just before they took me away. That was a lifesaving Christmas present."

The server brought their dinner to them and set the bowls on the table. Sadie scooped up a spoonful of stew, blew on it, and eagerly ate.

Troy saw how hungry she was. "When was the last time you ate something? I'm sorry, I didn't think to ask until now."

Sadie put her spoon down. Her eyes immediately welled up with tears. "It was all because of Eva that I had anything to eat at all. Let me back up. This part is going to be hard to hear, Troy. When she found me, she told me that we were going to run to her car that was parked on the side of the road. It was dark, and all I could see were the trees lit by a full moon. I panicked. I had an agoraphobic panic attack. If that hadn't have happened, maybe we would have escaped in time." She dabbed at her eyes with her napkin.

"Sadie, you're both safe now, and that's what counts. Keep in mind, you overcame your fears when you flagged us down on the road. You told us where Eva was."

"More coffee?" the server asked. She topped off both their cups then walked over to the next booth.

Sadie continued, "The man, the driver, hit Eva over the head. She was unconscious. He threw me in the fruit cellar. It wasn't too much later when he put her in there too. Eva opened jars of fruit for us to eat. She came up with a plan to escape. We would break a couple of wine bottles to use as weapons. When we heard him unlocking the door, we'd throw something at the lightbulb to shatter it so he'd be in the dark. We would be hidden on either side of the steps and cut him with the jagged glass when he came down. It worked out as planned. But he was able to get off a couple of shots at Eva. I ran, and he followed me to another house. I called 911 from there, but the phone went dead. I think he cut the line. At one point, I was able to hit him over the head with a vase. That gave me time to get away, and that's when you found me."

"I'm so sorry that you went through all that. You were very brave. Don't ever forget it."

They finished eating and decided to walk to the nurses' station to see if anyone had time to properly dress his wound. The nurse on duty stood when she saw him and put her hands on her hips. "Troy Winters, wasn't it just a few months ago that I told you I didn't want to see you back here again? Now what happened to you?"

"Uh-oh," Troy said with a sheepish grin.

"So, you're well-known here, I see." Sadie shook her head and laughed. "I'll be in the waiting room."

A half hour later, Troy was finished and joined Sadie. He was ready to sit down when Finn's shriek pierced the air.

"Mommy, you're okay!" His greeting of happiness was followed by Willow's voice. "Mom, I love you." Both children ran to her with their arms open wide. Finn jumped up on her while Willow contained herself enough to just put her arms around her mom and give her a strong hug.

"Kids, you're okay. I'm so glad to see you," she said while hugging and kissing them.

Troy watched as Sadie looked up into Oliver's eyes and the family reunited in a never-ending hug.

Chapter 40

Troy let Oliver know that he wanted to check in on Eva before they drove to the apartment. She was in room 502. He left the family in the waiting room and took the elevator up to the fifth floor. He found her room and walked in. There lay his beautiful wife of twelve years, on the bed with a breathing device around her mouth and nose, a needle in her arm, and hooked up to a monitor that read every breath, pulse, and heartbeat. A large bandage was on the side of her face.

Troy stood beside her bed and gently held her hand. He was amazed that she had risked her life for his sister. She was sleeping peacefully. "I love you, babe. I'll be back in the morning." He leaned in and kissed her on the forehead.

He turned and walked out, ready to be with his sister and her family for a good night's sleep in the downtown Portland apartment. After he joined them in the waiting room, they all got into Oliver's rented car and headed downtown.

"Uncle Troy, can I sleep with you?" Finn asked when they arrived, as if it was a campout or slumber party. Troy was amazed at how fast the kids rolled with the punches.

"Of course you can, Finn. How about we let your mom and dad have the bedroom and you and I camp out in sleeping bags on the living room floor. Willow can have the couch."

"Yay, I get to sleep with Uncle Troy!" Finn turned it into a song as he danced around the room.

Troy got out the bags, extra blankets, and pillows from the closet. Everyone gave each other good night hugs. Within half an hour, the apartment was quiet. Troy lay on the floor in one of the sleeping bags he and Eva had used on their last camping trip to the Sierra Mountains. It was only last September even though it seemed like so long ago. The bag still had the slight scent of the campfire they'd slept next to while falling asleep counting the stars. Those were good times. He tossed and turned. So many thoughts were going through his head that he found it hard to turn off the buzz and fall asleep. He realized how easily the events of the last couple of days could have gone in the wrong direction. He crawled out of the bag, took a couple of small pillows from a chair, and tucked them under his neck. He hoped they would help him get comfortable enough to sleep.

A soft light coming in from the edge of the curtains caused Troy to wake. He was surprised that he must have finally drifted off and glad that it wasn't a sleepless night. He had to keep his brain sharp for the events of the day. Anxious to see Eva, he got out of the sleeping bag and tiptoed into the bathroom to shower.

After Troy was dressed and ready for the day, the delicious smell of hot coffee coaxed him into the kitchen.

The coffeepot was filled with the brew, and Oliver sat at the table.

"Good morning, Oliver. Thanks for starting the coffee. How's Sadie doing?" Troy poured himself a cup.

"Surprisingly well. She fell asleep last night right away and is still sleeping like a baby."

"She went through a lot. I think she may have overcome her agoraphobia. She flagged us down in the dark while she was running down the road."

Oliver stood and refilled his cup. "I hope she has. I've heard of people who had faced their fears under extreme pressure and the phobia went away for good."

Willow walked in, covering a yawn with her hand. "Good morning, Dad and Uncle Troy." She gave them each a hug.

"Good morning, sweetie. You guys help yourselves to whatever you can find to eat around here. I'm going to rent a car and get over to the hospital to see Eva."

"We'll be down later today to visit her. Let me drive you to the rental office."

"Thanks, Oliver, but that's not necessary. We've got one just two blocks down the street, so I'll walk. It's one of the advantages of having an apartment in the city. Everything's close."

Troy said goodbye to them and went to get a car. While he walked, he thought about what he was going to do after checking on Eva. A phone call to Mike was high on his list. He was hopeful that they had either caught the bastard or had a definite lead on him. He wondered whether Gabe's body had been found. Even though Mike knew everything about the events that had happened, Troy would still have to file a statement with the police.

And Jasmine was probably wondering what was going on. He planned to call and let her know what had happened and see if everything was going well at the bed-and-breakfast.

Within forty-five minutes of leaving the apartment, Troy pulled into the parking lot of the hospital in his rented Chevy Malibu. He hurried to the elevator and punched the button for the fifth floor. He quietly walked into Eva's room. Her eyes were open.

"Troy, sweetheart. You're here." She reached toward him.

He kissed her on the forehead. "Babe, how are you feeling?"

"I've been better. It only hurts when I breathe, but I'll live."

"You better. You know I can't live without you."

"Did you guys catch the bastard?"

"Mike's on it. He was waiting for backup and Forensics to arrive at the lake last time I talked to him. I'll call him later and find out what's going on."

"And Sadie? How's she doing?"

"Everyone's okay, babe. The whole family is at our apartment right now. They got a good night's sleep and are planning on coming here to see you a little later."

The doctor walked in. He shook hands with Troy. "You know you have a very feisty wife, don't you?"

"Yes, sir, that's why I married her." Troy laughed.

"Eva, we've looked over your X-rays and decided to perform a surgical procedure called a rib plating. We'll realign the two ribs that were fractured and stabilize them by placing a titanium plate over them while they heal correctly. Would you like to talk this over with your husband first?"

"Sounds good to me. What do you think, babe?"

"I think a woman with a titanium plate in her chest sounds pretty sexy."

She laughed. "Aww, save your jokes for later, Troy. Breathing is hard enough right now. Laughing is too painful."

"Okay, Mrs. Winters, I'll see you soon in surgery." The doctor grinned and left the room.

Troy pulled a chair over to Eva's bedside, sat down, and held her hand. "My courageous wife, I sure do love you. By the way, thank you for saving my sister."

"Well, somebody had to do it." She smiled slightly. "Oh, when you talk to Mike, tell him the bastard took my Glock, and I want it back. He can keep my flashlight. My Buick is out there somewhere too."

"I'll do that, sweetheart. Don't you worry. All you need to do right now is heal. We'll take care of everything else."

A nurse entered the room, picked up Eva's chart, and checked it over. "Hi there. It looks like I need to get you prepped for surgery."

"Okay, I'll leave. I'll be here when you wake up." Troy kissed Eva's hand, stood up, and walked out the door.

He thought that the best place to make his phone calls would be from the privacy of his car. His first call would be to Mike.

"How are things going?" Troy asked when Mike answered the phone.

"Troy, yeah. We haven't found the guy yet. I just left the lake. I've been up there with Forensics all night. I just arrived at a café in a small town down the mountain. We found blood evidence in a boat that was tied up to the dock. We're assuming its Gabe Nolan's, and we have a team arriving anytime now to dredge the lake. We're trying to get an address on Adam Kent. How are the girls doing?"

"Sadie's remarkably fine, and Eva's doing great. She's going into surgery right now to put a couple ribs back together."

"Damn, that sounds bad."

"She wanted me to tell you that the bastard took her Glock and she wants it back."

Mike laughed. "Sounds like something she'd say. You can let her know that it's been found, and I told Forensics who the rightful owner was. I recognized it as Eva's. We'll make sure she gets it back. Her Buick was towed into the county's evidence garage. I knew that was hers, of course, even though the registration was missing."

"Okay, Mike, I'll let you go. Give me a call when anything else comes up."

"Gotcha."

His next call was to Jasmine. "Hey, girl. Just wanted to touch base. I haven't talked to you for a couple of days. Sadie and her family were in danger, but they're all safe and sound now."

"Thank God, Troy. I was worried."

"I know you were, and sorry I haven't called you before now. I guess I've been a little busy. Eva was involved in

Sadie's rescue. She caught a bullet and fractured a couple of ribs. She's in surgery right now and is doing just fine."

"Oh, Troy, I'm so sorry. You sure she'll be okay?"

"Yeah, she's a strong one. You know that."

"I sure do. It wasn't that long ago that both of you rescued me from that bastard Ross Conrad. I'll never forget that, and I'll always be grateful. What can I do for you two right now? There has to be something."

"Just keep doing what you normally do. It's a big help. Is everything going all right with the guests at the inn?"

"Oh, yeah, things are going great. Between the big breakfasts that I make and Sandy doing the cleaning, everything is running smoothly."

"Well, I really thank you for that. There is one thing, though. Would you ask Sandy if she would get one of her employees to go out to Sadie and Oliver's house and do a thorough cleaning? Forensics is finished with it, and I'd rather they didn't have any reminders of the trauma that went on there when they get home. Their address is in my book in the top drawer of my desk."

"I'll do that, Troy."

"Okay, I'll call you soon to let you know when we'll be home. It will be a few days."

"That's fine. Take care."

As soon as he hung up with Jasmine, his phone rang. Troy didn't recognize the number. "Hello."

"Hi, it's me, Oliver. I picked up a burner phone for now. Just wanted to call you to see how Eva was doing."

Troy let him know that Eva was in surgery and that he'd

give Oliver a call when she was awake and able to have visitors. Troy finished his calls and decided to go to the hospital's café, order breakfast, and wait.

Chapter 41

Adam woke to the sound of thunder. The trickle of rain outside his window soon turned into a downpour. Thunder and lightning followed.

What the hell?

It had slipped his mind to check the weather report. The last he'd heard, the unseasonably warm, dry weather was supposed to continue for a while. Adam knew the culvert was slightly above the ditch, but the way the rain was coming down, it could fill up soon, and then where would the water go? Logic told him that it would go into the culvert and soak the bags of money. They might even float out of their hiding place.

He couldn't believe he'd left them there in the first place. He shook his head and wondered what was wrong with him. He turned on the TV and clicked the remote until he got to the weather channel. Sure enough, there was an unexpected storm that might continue for the next few days.

Damn! Why am I so stupid?

He got dressed and grabbed his raincoat on the way out the door. Once he was in his car and on the road, he pounded on the steering wheel, still berating himself. The windshield wipers couldn't keep up with the deluge. Just yesterday, he'd thought his problems were over. He would keep the money well-hidden until it was time to leave.

Now there's another thing to deal with.

That was it—no more being patient, no more waiting. He would grab the bags, head for Florida, and take it from there. The more he planned, the worse things got.

Adam looked at the sky, and the storm was breaking up. At least that was something good. If the rain held off a little while, it would be easier to get the bags out. He drove a couple of miles out of town then turned onto the road where the money was hidden. He was getting close to the area when he saw a rural mail carrier's Jeep parked alongside the road exactly where the culvert was.

What the hell? What is he doing there?

Adam was furious. He drove past the Jeep a few feet and pulled over to the opposite side of the road. He didn't have his gun with him—he never thought he'd need it. He took the knife out of the glove compartment and tucked it in his pocket. He brought the raincoat's hood over his head and got out. When he crossed the road to see what was going on, the mail carrier was dragging one of the bags over to the back of the Jeep. He watched as the guy opened the door, lifted the bag, and threw it in. Adam saw that the other bag was already inside.

Who does he think he is?

Adam yelled, "Hey, what are you doing?"

The mailman threw the other one in then turned to him.

"I saw these bags sticking out of the culvert and thought they might be important. I grabbed them before they floated away. Why? Do you know something about them?"

"Yeah, they're mine. Hand them over."

"If they're so important, why were they in the culvert?"

"None of your damn business."

"Well, I think whatever is in them might be of interest to the cops. If they were hidden in a culvert, that means that you don't want anyone to know what they contain."

"Look, old man, throw them out on the ground and just drive away. I'm warning you."

The mail carrier stood his ground. "You're warning me? Look, you young punk, that's no way to talk. I got my shoes full of mud getting them out of the culvert. The least you could do is tell me what's inside."

"Like hell I will."

"I'll see for myself, then." He turned toward the bags and unzipped one. "Money? There's a lot of money in here. Where'd this come from?"

Adam pulled the knife from his pocket as he ran up to the man. He hooked his arm around the guy's neck and squeezed tight. He brought the knife up to the side of the man's face and touched the blade hard against his temple. A trickle of blood ran down the mailman's cheek.

"I'll say this once more. Throw the bags out on the ground and drive away. Now move it."

"Okay, okay, I'll do it. Just back off, man."

Adam's mind raced. He would have to kill the guy. The mailman could easily identify him and his car. The man had probably memorized his license plate number already. Adam would wait until the man threw out the second bag, then he'd stab him, slice his throat, and roll him off into the ditch. It could be hours before anyone found him. It wasn't unusual for a mail carrier's Jeep to be pulled off to the side of the road.

The mailman threw the first bag on the ground. As Adam reached down to pull it toward him, he heard the man grunt. Adam looked up just in time to see a tire iron coming at his head. The pain was sharp at first then dull and throbbing. He felt it multiple times, each one becoming less painful than the last. His vision darkened while bright pinpoints of light broke through the blackness. Adam felt the cold, wet grass against his face as he rolled down the slope of the ditch and sucked the muddy water into his lungs.

Chapter 42

Troy saw the police officer walking toward him as he sat in the waiting room of the hospital. He knew he would need to give a statement even though the bullet had only grazed him.

"Troy Winters?"

"Yes." He stood.

"Hi, I'm Officer Sam Fisher." He extended his hand. "State Trooper Michael Stevens said I'd probably find you here. He gave me most of the details of how both you and your wife received gunshot wounds, but I need to talk to each of you and have you sign a statement."

"Sure, I can answer any questions you may have. You'll have to wait until my wife is out of surgery to talk to her."

"Okay, do you mind if I record this?"

"I don't mind at all," he said.

They sat down, and Troy went over the details of the shots exchanged between him and Gabe.

"Any idea of the caliber of weapon he used?"

"Yeah, Forensics pulled a forty-five slug out of the kitchen wall. That was the one that grazed my shoulder. I was outside rolling on the ground when he fired off another round. That one, I was able to dodge, and then I returned fire."

"Do you know this man and where he is, or may be, at the moment?"

"From the information Sergeant Stevens and I were able to put together, we think he's deceased, and his name was Gabe or Gabriel Nolan. He's thought to be in the bottom of Lost Lake. They're searching for his body in there right now. My wife was shot at his cabin on that lake. We believe a man named Adam Kent was the one who shot her. As of this moment, we don't have concrete proof of any of this, but we should soon."

"Yes, Sergeant Stevens said the same. Do you have anything else to add at this time?"

"No, but it shouldn't be much longer. The details will be wrapped up soon."

Officer Fisher stood and thanked Troy for his statement. "I'll have this recording typed up and bring it along tomorrow for you to sign. I'll be back then to interview your wife if she's up to it."

"Thank you. I'll see you tomorrow."

Troy leaned his head back against the chair and closed his eyes. The physical and emotional events of the last couple of days were catching up with him. He felt bad that his wife and sister had gone through the hell that they had. Sadie should be okay. Maybe her panic attacks were gone for good. Oliver and the kids had gone through so much too. He wondered whether their ordeal would affect them emotionally for the rest of their lives. Eva was psychologically strong. That was a quality he'd noticed when he fell in love with her. She had never been shot before, though. He saw the desire for revenge in her eyes when she mentioned Adam Kent.

"Mr. Winters?"

Troy snapped out of his thoughts and saw the doctor standing in front of him. He jumped up. "Yes, how is she?"

"I'm pleased to tell you that your wife did just fine in surgery and is in the recovery room."

"Thanks, Doctor. That means a lot to me. When can I see her?"

"I'm sure she'll be asleep for a couple hours, but you can go sit with her anytime you want. Someone at the nurses' desk will tell you her room number."

"Thanks again. I appreciate all you've done."

Troy walked over to the nurses' station and asked for Eva's room number.

A nurse looked at her records. "She's in room 324."

"Thank you." Not wanting to wait for the elevator, Troy took the stairs two at a time. He found the room and walked in quietly. There she was, hooked up to tubes and needles. He pulled a chair up close and looked at her as she slept. Troy rubbed the top of her hand.

"I love you, my sweet Eva." He watched her for a few minutes then put his head down on the bed, closed his eyes, and fell asleep.

Chapter 43

Troy heard Eva calling his name. He woke and looked up into her eyes, and she had a slight smile on her lips.

"Do you want to crawl up here and sleep with me? You'll be more comfortable," she told him in a weak voice.

Troy laughed. "It was the sleep of a very relaxed husband. I was so relieved that you were okay. How do you feel, babe?"

"Like I've been shot in the ribs and then stabbed and sliced with a knife. Other than that, just fine."

A smile came across Troy's lips. "Good. Sounds like my girl."

A nurse walked into the room, greeted them, and began to adjust the IV and check Eva's vitals.

"I'll leave you alone for a little bit. I'll give Sadie and Oliver a call. I said I'd let them know when you were awake. They're anxious to see you."

Eva nodded, and he walked out to the waiting room to call Oliver.

"She's awake and doing fine," he told Oliver. "Just come to the waiting room. I'll meet you there, and we'll visit her together."

Oliver said they would be there soon. Troy went to the café, bought a large coffee, and walked to the waiting room. After taking a sip of the hot brew, he sat down to check for messages on his phone.

He had a text from Mike. It said he had the day off on Sunday and would drive Troy to Baker Flats if he wanted to pick up his Jeep. Troy tapped the contact and called him. "Hey, Mike. I got your message."

"How's Eva? Is she out of surgery?"

"She is, and doing fine, thanks for asking. Yeah, tomorrow would be a good time to go up there."

"Okay, I'll pick you up in the morning at nine. I've got a lot of information to fill you in on."

"Sounds good. See you then, thanks."

Troy had just finished his coffee and found a trash can to throw away the cup when he heard someone running up behind him. He turned to see Finn speeding toward him with his arms extended, ready for a hug.

"Uncle Troy!" He ran up to him and hugged his leg. "Is Aunt Eva okay?"

"She is, and she'll be so happy to see you guys. We'll go into her room and say hi, but we have to talk quietly and not stay too long. She needs her rest."

"Okay, I'll talk quietly."

Troy greeted the rest of the family, then they all went to room 324. Eva was still awake and smiled when she saw them.

"Hi, you guys. It's good to see you."

They all said their hellos and how glad they were that she

was okay. Sadie showed her the beautiful bouquet of flowers she had brought.

"What did they do to you in surgery?" Finn asked.

"Well, I had a couple of broken ribs that they put back together for me."

Finn looked confused. "How did they do that? You mean, like a puzzle?"

"They pushed them back together and then put a titanium plate over them to hold them in place."

"Wow, now you're kind of like a superhero."

Eva tried not to laugh, knowing it would hurt. "I hope so."

Sadie set the flowers on the side table for her. "She'll always be a superhero in our eyes."

Willow had made a get-well card for Eva and went up to the side of her bed and showed it to her. She had drawn a beach scene on the cover. Seagulls rested on the large rocks that jutted out of the ocean, and two kids were on the beach, flying a red kite. Inside, Willow had written, "This is what we want to do with you when you feel better and come home. Get well soon." They had all signed it.

Eva's eyes welled up with tears as she glanced at Troy and asked him for a tissue. He pulled one out of her box on the nightstand and handed it to her. "You know, Willow, that sounds like the most fun thing in the world. We'll all go to the beach for a day like this as soon as I'm feeling better."

Willow beamed as she set the card on the table, next to the flowers.

"We're so happy that you'll be okay, Eva. We'll let you

get some rest now," Oliver said. The family said their goodbyes, and Troy walked with them out of the room.

"Are you guys up for having dinner in the café before you leave?" Troy asked.

Oliver answered, "Sounds great. Sadie said the food was really good here."

They took the elevator to the café. Finn was happy that he got to push the down button. A corner booth was available, and they all squeezed in and looked over the menu. Oliver said he planned to order the beef stew since Sadie had raved about it, and everyone else wanted cheeseburgers and fries. Willow offered to place everyone's order with the server.

"Anything to drink?" the server asked.

"Oh, Mom, is it okay if we have sodas?"

"Sorry, hon, but I think milk would be better for you two."

"Okay, two glasses of milk, please."

The adults asked for coffee, and the server was quick to bring a pot over.

"Did the doctor say how long Eva would be here?" Sadie asked.

"He said that she did great with the surgery and in two to three days, she should be able to leave."

"That's good news. We were talking about going back home tomorrow morning unless you need us for anything here."

"Thanks for asking, but I'll be fine. My plan is to stay with Eva during the day and sleep at the apartment at night.

Oh, tomorrow morning, I'm going to ride up to Baker Flats with Mike to get my car. Would you guys stick around until I get back? I should return before noon."

Oliver nodded. "Sure, we'd be happy to. We'll come back to visit Eva and wait for you here."

"Thanks. I'd feel better if someone was close by in case she needs anyone. Mike said he'd let me know some of the details on the investigation. Forensics finished their work at the cabin."

"Uh, I think I have to go to the bathroom," Finn announced.

Willow offered to walk with him and wait outside the door.

"Thanks, Willow," Sadie said. She waited until they walked away then asked, "Forensics is finished at our house, aren't they?"

"Yes, they are," Troy said.

"When we get back, I hope the kids aren't immediately reminded of all the bad things that went on there. Children that young being tied up and held hostage is unthinkable, yet it happened. Surprisingly, they seem to be okay now."

"We're worried about emotional problems that may show up when they get home," Oliver said.

"I understand," Troy agreed. "Keep in mind, you guys could drive to our bed-and-breakfast and stay there until you feel okay about going back to your house. We have plenty of room. It's pretty empty this time of year."

Sadie touched Troy's hand. "Thanks, brother, really. We appreciate the offer, but that would just delay the situation. Keep in mind, I'll be in touch with my psychologist, so I'll be able to get her views on it."

"This morning, I contacted a security system company who will be out there Monday afternoon to install the latest equipment they have," Oliver assured them.

"I'm glad to hear that. By the way, I arranged for my housekeeper to send a couple of her employees out to your place to do a thorough cleaning. That way, there may not be immediate reminders of how the house looked when it all happened. But don't be surprised if you have two kids in bed with you guys for a while."

Sadie laughed. "That's true, and we'll welcome them in."

Chapter 44

The next morning, Troy woke before everyone else and drove a few blocks to drop off his rental car, then he enjoyed the crisp, fresh air on his walk to the apartment. Oliver was awake and drinking a cup of coffee when he returned. Troy filled a cup and joined him.

"I sure hope Mike has news that the coward has been caught," Oliver said.

"You and me both. I can't wait to see that bastard behind bars. I'm curious if the one who caught my bullet was found in the lake. The sooner they both never see the light of day again, the better."

Troy walked to the kitchen and looked at the street below. "There's Mike. He just pulled up and parked. Have a good morning, Oliver. I'll see you in a couple hours." He walked downstairs to his office and left from the front door.

"Hi. Thanks for doing this," he told Mike as he climbed in the front seat.

"Sure, anything to help. How's Eva and everyone else?"

"Amazingly well. Sadie and the family are going back home to Elk River today. I hope they can get their lives back to normal. So, what's the news?"

"Well, they found a body in the lake and identified him as Gabriel Nolan. He's in the morgue, and I'm sure they'll find a couple of your bullets in him."

"Good. Any luck in finding Adam?"

Mike gave him a sideways glance. "You're not going to believe this. His body was found in a ditch a couple miles from his apartment in Gold Mountain."

"What? You've got to be kidding. How? Who killed him?"

"All we know so far is that he was clubbed to death with a heavy blunt object. He had his wallet on him with his driver's license in it, and his Denali was parked across the road. A knife was found in the weeds, which suggests a confrontation went on. We're trying to pull prints from it."

"And the money?"

"Nope, his apartment has been searched—nothing."

"That's quite the turn of events. So adding this up, all three men that had something to do with the armored car robbery are dead, and the money has not been found?"

"You got it. Besides the few details our department is wrapping up, it's in the hands of the FBI now."

Troy shook his head in disbelief. They rode along in silence.

Fifteen minutes later, Troy saw the sign for Baker Flats. Mike took the exit. They began the climb in elevation.

"I forgot to ask you where Zak lives," Troy said. "Is he right here in town?"

"He's outside of town a few miles. I told him we'd meet

him at the café and that you'd buy him breakfast." Mike turned to him and smiled.

"Heck, I'll buy breakfast for both of you." Troy laughed.

They were coming into the main street of town when Troy saw his Jeep parked in front of the café. "Oh, good. He's already here."

They walked into the crowded building. Zak had saved a table for them, and he stood and waved them over. They all exchanged greetings and sat down.

"How are Eva and Sadie?" Zak asked.

"Thanks for asking. Eva took a bullet that went clear through her side and fractured a couple ribs on the way. She had surgery yesterday to get them aligned. She came out of it like a champ. Sadie's happy to be reunited with her family, and they're doing okay."

"Thank God. I'm so happy to hear that. Things were pretty bad last time I saw you."

"I'm forever in your debt for helping us find the place."

A pretty brunette with a cheerful smile walked up to their table and greeted them, handed out menus, and filled their cups with hot coffee.

"Our special of the day is a three-egg ham-and-cheese omelet with a side of our famous biscuits and sausage bacon."

"Honey, you got me as soon as you said biscuits," Zak told her.

"Sure. Got it, love."

"You can count me in," Troy agreed.

Mike continued with "Triple that."

"Three specials coming up. Oh, Zak, will you feed Scooter when you get home? I completely forgot this morning."

"Sure."

Mike and Troy looked at Zak quizzically.

"Yeah, she's my wife. I married well."

They laughed.

"From the look of all these people, this must be a pretty popular place," Troy said.

Zak grinned. "The only one in town."

"I guess that's true. They definitely have a monopoly on the café business here," Mike said.

"I don't know if you two are allowed to talk about it, but I'm curious if the men were caught," Zak said.

Mike answered, "From the details we've managed to put together, it seems like they're both deceased."

"Well, that's good. They won't be out there terrorizing others."

Zak's wife came over with the coffeepot, ready to refill their cups. "Your plates are coming right up, boys."

"So Zak, how long have you lived in this area?" Troy asked.

"I was born right here. My mother gave birth to me in a small house on the edge of town. I figured why leave? Lots of good fishing and hunting around. Although Tilly, my wife, would like to get away and go on a vacation somewhere. I'll think of something. She certainly deserves it."

Tilly appeared with the plates of hot food. The hungry trio wasted no time digging in.

"You know, Zak, Eva and I have a beautiful bed-and-breakfast inn a few hours from here on the coast. It sits up on a bluff overlooking the ocean in the small town of New Haven. Have you heard of it?

"Oh yeah, I went there a couple times with my family when I was a kid. Those days at the beach were fun times. It's been many years, though. I bet things have changed."

"Well, I would be honored to have you and Tilly come and stay in one of our suites. It would be a great vacation for you both, and it would be complimentary. My thanks to you for helping us out the other day and to Tilly for such great service."

"Thanks, that would be a kick. We'd both love that."

When they finished their breakfasts, Troy paid the bill and waved at Tilly as they walked out to their cars.

Mike went to his car, got a box out from the back seat, and gave it to Troy. "Your Sig Sauer, my friend."

"Hey, Mike, thanks, and I appreciate the ride up here. We'll talk soon."

Mike said goodbye to them both and drove away.

"Hop in, Zak. I'll give you a ride home."

They drove three miles out of town and Zak had him turn left into a driveway. A small, well-kept house sat on the property. A red barn stood behind it, and a horse ran up to the fence when Troy stopped the car.

"Oh, Thunder is ready for his morning apple."

"Nice place. How many acres do you have?"

"Fifteen for now. I might purchase a few more soon. My neighbor's selling out."

Troy opened the console and took out a business card.

"Here's my card. Give me a call when you and Tilly are ready for that vacation. We'd love to have you."

"Will do. Thanks, Troy."

On the way to Portland, Troy let his mind wander and thought about the extreme differences in people. Some were out to give their fellow man a helping hand with anything they needed, whether they knew them or not. Others thought only of themselves. They wanted to become rich no matter what the cost. They justified their greed by taking the lives of others and, then in the end, lost their own.

Chapter 45

Troy woke in a happier mood than he had been in for a while. It was Tuesday morning, the day that Eva would be released from the hospital and go home. He showered, made breakfast, and cleaned up around the apartment. Not knowing when he would be there again, he threw out the leftover food in the refrigerator and locked up tight on his way out the door. At least for the next few weeks, he wouldn't take on any investigations. Spending time with Eva while she healed was more important.

The drive to the hospital took only fifteen minutes. Traffic was unusually light that morning. He parked his Jeep and hurried up to her room. There she was—his lovely wife sitting up in the bedside chair with a smile on her face.

Troy laughed when he saw her. "You're not anxious to leave here, are you?"

"You better believe I am. Take me home, babe."

Her nurse walked in and gave her instructions for recovery before saying goodbye.

"Remember, take it easy for six weeks. Wear your brace when you're walking. Put ice packs against your side a couple times a day for a duration of fifteen to twenty minutes. No heavy lifting and practice your deep breathing exercises. Do you have your pain meds with you?"

"Yes, ma'am." Eva grinned. "I'd give you a hug if I could. Maybe next time. You know I'm going to miss you, don't you?"

"I'm going to miss you, too, but I better not see you here again," her nurse said as she helped Eva into a wheelchair.

Troy added, "If I have anything to do with it, she definitely won't be back. Thanks for taking such good care of her."

Troy walked ahead of them to get the Jeep and parked close to the hospital door. He and the nurse helped Eva into the car then said their goodbyes.

"Do you need anything at the apartment before we get on the road?" Troy asked.

"Not that I can think of. I just want to go home. I miss the view from the balcony. If this beautiful weather holds out, I plan on spending a lot of time lying on a chaise with a cozy blanket and watching the waves come in."

"Home it is." He stepped on the gas and headed for I-5.

Troy touched the radio buttons until he found a station playing soft jazz. "I forgot to ask, how do you feel today?"

"I think I'm healing fairly well. I have less pain than I did yesterday. As long as I don't laugh or cough, I have it made." She gave Troy a stern look. "So none of your jokes for a while, mister."

"Who, me?" He grinned. His phone sat on the console between them, and when it sounded, he glanced at the screen. "It's Mike. You want to get it?" He reached over to turn the music down.

Eva picked it up and put it on Speaker. "Hey, Mike, it's Eva. Troy and I are on our way home, and I've got you on Speaker."

"Eva, hi. I'm so glad you're headed home. How are you?"

"Not too bad. I told Troy as long as I don't laugh, nothing hurts."

"Well, good thing you're talking to me, then. I never have anything funny to say." He laughed. "I just thought I'd call to let you both know the rest of the details of the case and how it wrapped up on our end. Eva, I'm sure Troy has filled you in about finding Adam Kent's body and the other facts that we knew last time I talked to him."

"Yes, he did. The coward got what he deserved. We just wondered who killed him since Lucas and Gabe were already dead."

"That, we don't know. A truck was reported abandoned at a motel just a few miles from Sadie and Oliver's house. It was registered to Gabe. They rented adjoining rooms on Christmas Eve under false names. They must have made their last-minute plans there and left for your sister's house in Adam's Denali. Gabe was in no condition to drive his truck back, so they just left it there. The fillet knife found in the weeds was checked for fingerprints and blood traces. The blood was Gabe's, and the fingerprints were Adam's. So it looks like someone else knew about the money, a confrontation happened involving the knife and a blunt object, and Adam lost. The FBI has complete control of the case now. They want to find the money."

Troy asked, "Did Gabe's body have knife wounds?"

"Yeah, four deep ones, right in the chest."

"Wow, brutal."

"Yep, those two were monsters. Anyway, I've got good news for you, Eva. We're sending two officers over to the inn with your Buick and Glock. I'll have them leave late this afternoon so you'll be home to receive them. A hunting knife found in the cabin has your initials carved in the handle. As soon as I saw it, I remembered that Troy gave it to you as a gift years ago. We'll return that too."

"Thanks, Mike. We appreciate all you do," Eva said. "Expect a dinner invitation as soon as I'm feeling better."

"I'll look forward to it. Take care."

After ending the call, Troy asked her if she thought she'd be ready to cook for company anytime soon.

"No, but Jasmine's great at it." Eva smiled, put her head back, and closed her eyes and rested.

Troy turned the soft music back on, exited I-5, and headed west. He was eager to get home.

His phone sounded again. It was Jasmine, so he put her on Speaker and said hello.

"Hi, Troy. Are you guys on your way home?"

"We are and looking forward to getting there."

"That's great. I'm making a big pot of clam chowder, salad, and garlic toast. I just wanted to make sure."

"You don't know how good that sounds. We all know you make the best clam chowder. We should be there in about an hour."

"Okay, see you guys soon."

Enjoying the scenic drive along the winding road, Troy was glad to be out of the city. He always enjoyed being there at first, but after a few days, he was ready to get back to where life was slower.

Eva stirred and turned to him. "I must have fallen asleep. The pain pills are pretty strong."

"You're doing just what you need to do. Rest is important." He reached over and held her hand. "Have I told you today how much you mean to me?"

"Not for a couple of hours at least." She smiled. "I love you, babe."

Soon, they pulled into their quaint little town of New Haven and drove up the bluff road to the inn. After Troy pulled in and parked, Jasmine ran out to greet them.

"Eva, I'm so happy to see you. Here, let me help you into the house."

Troy got out and went around to her side of the car, and with the assistance of both of them, Eva got safely inside.

She sat down on the couch and covered her legs with a soft blanket. Jasmine excused herself to check on dinner, and Troy built a fire in the fireplace. He twisted newspaper and set kindling on top of it. "It will get nice and toasty here in a few minutes," he said as he lit a match and watched the flames start to grow.

"Mm, home sweet home." Eva tucked a pillow against her side.

Troy heard a couple of vehicles pull into the driveway. He looked out the window and saw an officer get out of Eva's

Buick while carrying a box. A patrol car was parked behind it.

"The officers are here with your car. I'll go out and talk to them."

He walked outside and greeted them. "Hi, guys. I'm Troy Winters. Thanks for driving my wife's car here."

"You're welcome. I have a box containing a Glock and a knife with a leather sheath. Can you identify them?"

Troy looked in the box. "Yes, they're both my wife's."

He signed for them, thanked the officers, and went back in the house with the box and car keys. "Honey, your car, gun, and knife are here," he said in a singsong voice.

"That's a statement you don't hear every day. Thanks, babe."

Jasmine brought out a tray of hot cocoa for them and sat on the couch next to Eva. "So are you in a lot of pain?"

"You know, it's not too bad right now. The pain pills are helping. It was a pretty involved surgery. I'll take it easy for about six weeks, and then I should be back to normal. How are things going around here?"

"We've got Don and Cici Shearer from Colorado staying for a few days, and Adeline and Thomas Murphy are leaving in the morning. They're here from Maine. They like our coast better than theirs in the winter."

Troy laughed. "I can see why. I like snow when I want to ski, but other than that, they can keep it."

"Both couples have reservations in town for dinner, so you might not be able to meet them until tomorrow morning."

Eva asked, "Anyone coming in next week?"

"Just a couple from Arizona arriving next weekend. It's the slow season. Good time for you to relax and heal. Well, dinner's almost ready. Do you feel like coming to the table, or would you like me to bring a couple trays out here?"

"If you don't mind, it would be great to eat out here by the fire. Thanks."

"That sounds good. I'll give you a hand." Troy stood and walked to the kitchen with Jasmine.

She took the salads out of the refrigerator, slid the tray of garlic bread under the broiler, and glanced at Troy. "She really had a close call. Thank God she's okay. How bad is the wound on her cheekbone?"

Troy filled the soup bowls with clam chowder. "It looked pretty bad when I found her. I'm not sure how many stitches she had. It will be her choice whether she wants to have cosmetic surgery in the future."

"Well, it's good to have you both home. I'm glad Sadie and her family got through it all too. You have a lot of strong people in your family."

"Thanks for your concern. We feel that you're part of our family too. Remember, it wasn't that long ago that your life was in danger. You got away from that maniac, Ross Conrad, because of your strength and ingenuity."

Jasmine smiled. "Don't forget that you and Eva had a lot to do with my rescue."

They took the food to the living room and set everything on tray tables. Troy put a couple of logs on the fire.

"Jasmine, this is delicious. It's so creamy and full of flavor." Eva dipped the edge of the crispy bread into the bowl.

"Thanks. I had fun shopping for the fresh ingredients down in Old Town today. Everyone was in such a great mood. They were all getting ready for the celebration tonight."

"Celebration?" Troy looked up at her from his bowl of soup.

"What celebration?" Eva cocked her head.

Jasmine looked at them both and shook her head in disbelief. "I'll be right back." She got up and walked toward the kitchen.

Troy looked at Eva and shrugged. Five minutes later, Jasmine was back in the room, carrying a round tray with three champagne glasses on it.

"I know you two have had your minds on other things lately, and I don't think either of you will be staying up till midnight, so Happy New Year!"

Troy laughed, and Eva tried not to. She gave Jasmine a big smile instead.

"Well, that's a first. We've never forgotten New Year's Eve before," Eva said.

Jasmine gave them each a glass. "Eva, yours is filled with sparkling water. Pain pills and alcohol don't mix."

"That's true. I'll wait and enjoy my champagne in a few weeks with my Sunday morning mimosa."

Troy stood and held up his glass. "Cheers, to my lovely wife and wonderful friend. May next year be full of healthy and happy days."

They clinked their glasses together while the warm glow of the crackling fire filled the room.

Chapter 46

The First Day of Spring

Eva took her spot on the balcony and lay down on her favorite chaise lounge. Perfect weather. Perfect view. The puffy white clouds stood out against the deep-blue sky and reminded her of a Maxfield Parrish painting. The foam-tipped waves gently broke against the rocks. The scene alone was mesmerizing.

Eva heard footsteps behind her and opened her eyes to see her sweet husband leaning in for a kiss. "Good morning, love." She smiled softly.

"Good morning to you. How'd you sleep?"

"Like a baby."

He handed her a cup of coffee. "Here you go. Your favorite brew, French roast."

"Thanks, babe. How is everything downstairs? Are the guests up yet?"

"Rita and Jack O'Leary are out on the veranda, drinking coffee. Jasmine has breakfast almost ready, and Zak and Tilly should be in the dining room soon."

"I'm glad you invited them. They sure are a fun couple to be around. Tilly seems overjoyed to be here."

Troy sat on a chair next to her and sipped his coffee. "Yeah, they are a great couple. I don't think they leave home much, so this is pretty special to them."

"What time will Sadie, Oliver, and the kids be here?"

"They said it would be around one o'clock."

"Did you buy the red kite?"

"I sure did. I got the tail and string on it this morning. We'll make an afternoon of it. Everyone on the beach for a walk and the kids flying a red kite, just like in Willow's drawing. I saw that you put the card she made for you downstairs on the table."

Eva reached for his hand. "Yeah, I guess I'm sentimental that way. I love the way kids have that inner spirit in them, like they know that everything will be fine after a little bit of time passes. She was right."

Troy looked into her eyes. "Maybe we should have a couple of our own. Willow and Finn would be their cousins. Can't ask for better relatives than that."

She gave him her special smile. "Hmm, something to think about. Ready to go downstairs and have one of Jasmine's award-winning breakfasts?"

He took hold of her arm and helped her up. "You don't have to ask me twice."

They walked downstairs together and joined the guests in the dining room.

"Good morning, everyone," Eva said. "Jasmine has set everything out on the buffet table. Please help yourselves."

The O'Learys started the line with Zak and Tilly following. Eva walked into the kitchen to see if Jasmine needed any help.

"Thanks, Eva. I think I've got it. If you carry out the creamer and sugar bowl, I'll grab the carafe of coffee."

They all filled their plates and took a seat at the long mahogany table.

"Happy spring equinox, everyone," Jasmine reminded them.

"That's right, we've got approximately twelve hours of both daylight and darkness today. We can look forward to longer days for a while," Troy reminded them.

"More beach time." Tilly laughed. "You know we'll have a hard time leaving here. This has been such a relaxing vacation."

Zak pitched in, "Yeah, we decided that we're coming back here every year. This has been great. It's a wonderful change of scenery."

The O'Learys agreed and said they would be back too. "The beach walks and ocean breezes are invigorating. Although we love our farm in Kansas, we'll have to come back here as often as we can. We're addicted," Jack said.

Eva passed the basket of muffins around the table. "Help yourselves to more if you'd like. We have family coming over this afternoon for kite flying and a long walk on the beach. We'd love to have all of you join if you'd like. We'll be the crazy-looking family under the red kite."

The guests laughed and agreed to go.

After breakfast, Eva helped Jasmine clear the table and

get the dishes in the dishwasher. She was wrapping up leftover ham slices when she told Jasmine about a class that was beginning soon. "Did I tell you that Sadie and I are going to sign up for a women's self-defense class?"

"What? How exciting. Where is it going to be held?"

"In Old Town at the community building. It starts next week. We want you to take it with us."

"Sure, I'm in. That's something we should have done a long time ago. All three of us have been abused, beaten, shot at, and taken hostage. Yeah, let's hope we never have to demonstrate any kind of physical defense in our future, but learning how to, just in case, is an excellent idea."

"Good, sign-up is tomorrow at noon. Lunch is on me after that. Oh, and Troy taught me how to hot-wire a car."

"Really? Good, now you can teach me." Jasmine laughed.

Eva poured two glasses of iced tea and asked Jasmine to join her on the veranda. "The tide is coming in, and we can watch the sand labyrinth wash away."

They leaned against the railing and looked down at the beach. The designs and circles that

had been drawn in the sand were still visible but slowly disappearing with each gentle wave.

Off in the distance, a man leaned against a sea stack, holding a controller in his hands. "Oh look, Jasmine, it's Jason. He must be flying his drone nearby." They yelled down to him and waved. He looked up and held his hand up high. It wasn't long until they heard the low hum of the drone coming toward them. They had to laugh when it flew within a few feet of them, and the words *Hi There* were painted on the front of it along with a big yellow smiley face. Jason made the drone's wings tip up and down in a wave goodbye, then just as fast as it appeared, it flew off in the direction of the ocean.

When she heard loud, excited voices, Eva turned toward the house. Finn came running out of the door, clearly eager about the kite-flying day.

"Aunt Eva, we're here!" he yelled, full of energy.

"I see that." She laughed and gave the little guy a hug.

"Hi, Jasmine. Are you going with us to fly the kite?"

"You know, Finn, I wouldn't miss it for the world."

The family took the bluff trail down to the beach. Oliver and Troy led the way and got the kids started on getting the kite up.

"Run, Willow, run!" Finn yelled to his sister. They all watched as the bright-red kite, backlit by the sun, left the sand and twirled, rising high in the air.

The kids took turns holding the reel of string and maneuvering the kite. The family and friends continued to walk south along the water's edge, trying to outrun the waves as the tide came in, splashing at their toes.

A yellow lab ran after a Frisbee, swooped past Eva, and retrieved the Frisbee just as it hit the water, spraying salt water all over her. She recognized the dog as Harper, her four-legged friend. Her owner, eight-year-old Maddex, couldn't be too far away. Eva decided to sit on a driftwood log and rest while she watched the activity around her. Harper ran past with the Frisbee in tow, searching for her owner. Then Eva heard Maddex's voice.

"Harper, Harper, come here, girl."

Eva looked south, and Maddex ran out from behind a sand dune. It had been a while since she had spent any time on the beach with him. He was her treasure-collecting buddy, and she noticed how much he had grown since last fall. She held her hand up high and waved.

"Hi, Eva, I haven't seen you for a long time. Where have you been?" He ran up to her with a canvas bag in hand. Harper followed, dropped the Frisbee on the ground, and sat next to her.

"Uh, well, I had an accident and had to have my ribs adjusted."

"Are you better now?"

"I am. I'm a lot better."

"You have a big cut on your cheek. Did you have stitches?"

"Yes, I did. I could have the scar removed later with another surgery. Do you think I should?"

He squinted, tilted his head, and studied her for a moment. "No, you should leave it like it is. I think it makes you look cool, like no one would want to mess with you."

Eva gave it some thought and smiled. "That's an interesting point of view. Thanks. What kind of treasures have you found today?"

"You won't believe it." He opened his bag. "Look, I found two agates and a piece of petrified wood. Hold one up to the light. You can see through it. That's how you know it's an agate."

She held one up to the sky and was amazed at its clarity.

"Look at Harper. She's looking up at it, too, but she probably thinks it's a treat. And now, for the best surprise. Are you ready?"

Eva nodded. "Yep."

"Close your eyes." He opened his bag and dug around. "Okay, you can open them now."

She did and saw that he was holding up a large piece of beach glass. It was orange, and the edges were smooth from years of being tossed around in the ocean. "That's beautiful. I've never seen an orange one."

"That's because it's the rarest color. It's the first time I've ever found one like this."

He leaned against Eva's shoulder and held his treasure up high. The bright sun twinkled through it as they looked at it in awe.

"What if the whole world was made out of beach glass?" he asked her.

She put her arm around him. "What if, Maddex? What if?"

THE END

I hope you enjoyed *Dead Man's Money*, the second book in the Troy and Eva Winters Private Investigation Thriller Series.
Thank you!

If you have a minute to spare, I would love it if you would post a short review. It would be appreciated and will help others discover my books.

Find all my books in the Troy and Eva Winters series at http://kjnorth.com

Sign up for my newsletter at: http://kjnorth.com/newsletter/ There, you'll find release dates for my newest books and information on fun raffles that I'll be offering with every book launch.

You can find me on Facebook at
https://www.facebook.com/kjnorthauthor/

Made in the USA
Middletown, DE
09 September 2024

60044543R00149